Published in Gr

The Anansi A

www.anansiarchive.co.uk

Copyright remains with authors

All rights reserved.

This book or any portion thereof maybe not be reproduced without express written permission of the publisher except for brief extracts in reviews.

This anthology is entirely a work of fiction and any similarity to characters, descriptions and details portrayed is entirely coincidental. Any opinions herein are those of the author and not the publisher.

Cover:

Special thanks to Danni Jordan for

making this book possible

CONTENTS

Foreword..7

SHORT FICTION

THE BLOODHEAD TRAIL

By Elaine Rockett..9

CONFESSIONS OF A CLOCK-WALKER

By Lucia Kali...21

SOCIAL SHADE

By James Dwyer..30

CAROLINA

By Leslie Roberts..38

THE UNQUIET GRAVE

Becca Brown..48

BAD CHOICES

By Philip Gibson..56

CRIMSON FOR CRIMSON

By Adam Shakinovsky……………………………………..69

A GIFT FROM THE SEA

By Caroline Quigley……………………………………….82

A STRANGER'S LOOKOUT

by Charlotte West……………………………………….89

A SPOON IN THE SOCKET

by Kit Derrick………………………………………..……..97

WIDOWED

by Ian Carass…………………………………………..…...106

LAST NIGHTS OF THE PANTO

by Tabitha Bast………….………………..………......…..112

FEARLESS

by Lesley Aldridge……………………………………..…120

THE WHEELS MUST KEEP TURNING

by Warren Tang………………………………………….125

FORTIETH

by Ed Walsh…………………………………………….133

TURNING OF THE TIDE

By Wanda Dakin…………………………………………..141

FLASH FICTION

BABY LOVE

By Ellen Evers……………………………………………..151

JACKSON CREEK

By Gail Warrick Cox………………………………….....153

OKAY TEACHER!

By Oluwatimilehin Oladiran ………………..………..…..155

A COLD CONDOLENCE

By John Blair……………………………………….....…..157

TITLES

By Patsy Collins…………………………………………..160

POETRY

ODE TO AFFLICTION

By Aisling McEvoy……………………………….…..……..163

THE LITTLEST WITCH

By Dawn Rae...165

SILENCE

By Emily Raisin...167

VEGETAL WOMAN

By Kenzie Packer..169

BIRTH OF A NIGHTINGALE

Ece Karadag...170

A PRAYER TO BABBITT

by Fiorella Ruas..172

TO BE HELD BY LIGHT

By Lesley Mason...173

WORKING NINE NINE SIX

by Creana Bosac...177

THERE'S STILL TIME TO BE CREATIVE?

By S.R. Malone...179

STARFISH

By Heather Haigh..182

WE NOW ACKNOWLEDGE

By Sandra Achebe..184

UNTO THE WATERS

By Sarah Edwards..186

SKY

By R.J. Finnerty..189

PHOENIX

By Finlay J. Goodwin...190

PHANTOMS

By Ursula O'Reilly..191

ONE

By Louise Hastings..193

ALL-CONSUMING NIGHT

By Amelie Addison..194

PERSPECTIVE

By Faith McCormick..196

Foreword

Welcome to our eclectic and somewhat lop-sided fourth edition in the Anansi Archive anthology series.

Lop-sided? In the most elegant of worlds we would find a perfect harmony between the number of short, flash fiction and poetry contributions. Alas, such elegance bears the fingerprints of forced design and our model is not like that.

Our job is take only the cream of contributions and if that means a dominance of short fiction and poetry, then so be it. So what has happened to the craft of brevity?

Flash fiction is a writing art form all its own and there's plenty of advice freely available on how it works and why it often doesn't. Suffice to say that authors must treat each of their precious 500 words with the care of a micro-surgeon and the ruthlessness of an autocrat.

In a world where so many talkers have little to say or their point it is lost in the landfill of verbiage, the art of concision is struggling for breath. It is the skill of seeing words as precious stones being placed in a stunning piece of jewellery. And it is the art of knowing when to stop.

It is an absolute delight to welcome contributions in this anthology from Africa, a continent under-represented in previous editions. Our global reach continues to inspire us as we hope this collection does you.

Dave Jordan, Editor   **October 2022**

Short Fiction

THE BLOODHEAD TRAIL

By Elaine Rockett

It was prophetic, calling their bald afterthought Ruby simply because they liked the name. She began sprouting wavy vermilion hair and her mousy-haired mother would turn to her similar-hued husband and exclaim: "She's not like us, is she?"

She wasn't. One massive bone of contention was Ruby's family's sporting prowess. Her father pulled on his trainers for a daily jog in all weathers, playing tennis frequently. Her mother attended aerobics and gymnastics, and frequently boasted of how she'd been chosen for the town sports in her youth, a feat both Ruby's brothers (also rodent-haired and quite a bit older than her) achieved each year.

But Ruby was hopeless at sport. Unable to throw, catch or hit a ball, she was slung out of P.E. at school for being useless, and came last in all her races on sports day. Sundays, they'd cycle out as a family to the local field to play games which Ruby would inevitably ruin with her propensity to wallop a ball away if it was thrown at her to catch.

Their yearly holiday camp sojourn was the worst. Her father would sign the whole clan up for activities like quad biking, volleyball or badminton, resulting in crotchety wailing from a reluctant Ruby, usually scabbed and bruised from whatever she'd managed to fail at the day before.

But here she stuck her heels in. She wanted to attend the art workshop and was damned if she was going to let these idiots stop her in favour of an hour falling over on roller skates. Her brothers scowled: "Bloodhead!", throwing the ball at her head as she sat down to make a daisy chain, stubbornly interrupting their game. But Ruby smiled as she rubbed her skull, liking the moniker.

Ruby wasn't just a lover of drawing. Her dad had an old pictorial atlas - one with countries she knew were now renamed, such as Ceylon, Persia and Rhodesia - and she spent hours examining it, tracing her fingers over exotic photos of the Sahara Desert, wondering what it was like to live there. As she got older she imagined herself like Scheherazade; riding barefoot across undulating sands on a camel, veiled and mysterious, or wandering into the pyramids then sailing down the Nile like a cursed heiress from an Agatha Christie plot.

They frequently visited her mother's extended family on their council estate, but there was one family member they rarely saw. "Been married four times!" Barbara shook her head; cocooned within her backward morals.

Once she was cycling, Ruby's father took her to the outskirts of town to meet her paternal granny. Ruby found this statuesque, patrician woman, fascinating. She always wore black - often a severe dress, although trousers when tending her garden - but still drove; her little white Mini Metro parked alongside her cute, picture-postcard cottage. Local folklore dictated that she was a witch; a reputation which no doubt sprang from her ownership of a black cat, a rustic broom and a cauldron for cooking her fragrant, self-grown vegetable soups. She had titian hair as well; although hers now had huge white streaks running through it, like road lines.By the age of eleven Ruby frequently took off to see her granny, usually finding her outside in the garden which veered down towards the confluence of the rivers, intrigued as to why her parents hardly ever saw her.

"Call me Gwen. Short for Gwendolyne. Granny makes me sound old!" she insisted, in plummy vowels unlike her mother's but similar in tone to her father's.

"Doesn't that name come from Guinevere?" Ruby said, always eager to impress adults with her superior knowledge. Pretentious, her mother had labelled her, but Gwen laughed and raised a pencilled eyebrow, rather liking the rebellious nature of this little outcast.

"Drinkie?" Gwen possessed a huge physical globe on a stand, which had attracted Ruby's attention from the offset. She stared in amazement as Gwen manoeuvred the lid to reveal a myriad of bottles nestled inside, like soldiers. She nodded, getting the impression that it was not orange squash she was being offered, and Gwen poured, squinting and adding a few drips of something which turned the concoction pink.

Ruby sipped her gin and tonic, the crisp alcohol giving her a lovely, soft fuzzy head. "Mum and Dad don't drink. Ever."

Gwen scowled, exasperated. "That's Boring Barbara's influence." Then she looked contrite. "I'm sorry. I know she's your mother. But she's so... modulated. She could have represented her country in gymnastics - freestyle, floor acrobatics. But did she? No, because she thought it best to leave school and work in a factory shelling peas, like her small-town, narrow-minded family wanted."

"It's where Mum and Dad met."

"Humph. I know." Gwen slotted a pastel coloured cigarette into a holder, lighting it with a chunky pewter lighter. "All that money wasted on a private education for him to work as a bookkeeper. In a factory. Ambitionless Aubrey. That's what she turned him into."

Gwen later elaborated, smirking ironically as Ruby shared her ambitions of travelling. "I didn't want children, you know," she gave Ruby a concentrated stare.

Ruby reddened, but she was well-read enough to understand and preened, inordinately pleased that Gwen saw her fit to confide in.

"There were ways and means, even back in the thirties. I used the Dutch cap. Until my first husband," Gwen never mentioned him by name "found it and beat me. I wasn't going to put up with that so I left him, much to the scandal of my family, who temporarily disowned me."

"Come," she took Ruby up neat spiral stairs, pulling open a heavy wardrobe on the landing, presenting a glittering rainbow of dresses, feather boas and heels; clearly old-fashioned but extremely well-preserved. Gwen laughed, and for a second the timbre of her voice took on a high-pitched nuance, like that of a much younger woman as she recited the designers of her clothing. "Vionnet. Paquin. Schiaparelli. Coco Chanel. I rented a flat with another girl and took a job as a nightclub singer, travelling up to London on the Tube - we're at the end of the line, as you know. I sometimes stayed out all night..." she winked at Ruby, who got the gist and grinned conspiratorially. "Then..." she looked wistful, "..the war started. I remarried - of course it was lust. My contraception failed, I had your father. He never met his father- he died fighting. Well, I drove ambulances, for the ATS," she shrugged. "By then Mama was widowed and she looked after Aubrey."

At home Ruby's frequent visits were questioned outright, so she raised the issue in Gwen's refreshingly light and modern sitting room, prompting her to elaborate. "They said I'm after your money..."

"Ha!" Gwen said, walking outside and passing a trowel over to Ruby. "They think I'm loaded, coming from the upper class- impoverished though it was."

"They reckon you've got more jewels than the Queen..."

Later, when they'd finished planting and rinsed the pungent smell of rosemary off their hands, Gwen padded upstairs and returned holding a thick photo album, continuing the conversation. "They're stupid. How d'you think I paid for Aubrey's upbringing? His education? How do you think I paid for this place? I sold 'em."

"They said it was your fourth husband's house, and that you married him for it." Ruby smiled, vaguely remembering kind Ted, who'd continually sucked on Murray mints; removing a half-eaten sweet and secreting it in his handkerchief whenever he was called to the dinner table.

Gwen shook her head sadly. "Rot! It's always been my house, and I married him for companionship."

"They reckon you've buried all your jewellery in your garden..."

Gwen laughed incredulously. "One day they caught me unawares, burying my furs. I came to realise that killing animals is wrong, so I started wearing fake. And I thought the dead animals deserved a proper burial so I buried 'em outside, in the same way I buried Winston, Queenie and Tabitha." Ruby refrained from referring to the chewy roast beef sandwiches they'd devoured for lunch."

"They said they're going to dig up the garden once they inherit your cottage..."

"Good luck to them!" Ruby never mentioned what was discussed at the cottage with her parents, although they mined her for information.

"They say you like..." Ruby was unsure how to word this, "...men of colour."

Gwen's eyes grew wistful and she turned sharply. "Saïd," her voice was very low. "They mean Saïd. The true love of my life."

Gwen then flapped her arms, surprising Ruby by asking her to leave; something she'd not done before. Although stung by the rejection, on the way home Ruby rolled the foreign name around her tongue, for effect. Saïd...

It was some months before Gwen talked about her love again. "It was not his real name. And, like Heathcliff, he tended to use only the one name serving as both Christian and surname." She quizzed Ruby, "Do you know what an Emir is?"

Ruby shook her head so Gwen told her. "It means prince. Saïd was a Saudi Arabian prince."

Ruby was obviously impressed, but noted how Gwen's whole demeanour became guarded as she embarked upon this subject. "He had to leave after the territorial merger of 1932. There were problems with family affiliations," Gwen said carefully, picking at unseen cottons hanging from her dress, "so his mother granted him access to their bank vaults. He cleared it of money and jewellery and left. I met him at the end of the war - I still popped down to London whenever I could. I remember him just sitting alone in a jazz bar, exhaling cigarette rings into the air like a magician."

She looked at Ruby intensely. "I can't explain how I felt that first time we locked eyes - it was like spiralling down into a vortex. It'd never happened before and it's never, ever happened since," Gwen said candidly. "We were married five weeks later." She winked at Ruby. "Of course, it didn't hurt that he was devastatingly, hypnotically attractive but yes, he was an Arab. He was a 'man of colour' as your mother so succinctly puts it.

He'd claimed asylum here and had returned his debt to the British government by undertaking very important top secret work during the war. But he couldn't tell me about it, or his previous name, so I remained ignorant of the details. But I did know that he was Saudi royalty. As do Boring Barbara and Ambitionless Aubrey. Or, maybe I should rename him Avaricious Aubrey. We put Aubrey in," she smiled thinly, "a very expensive boarding school and set about travelling the world. First class."

Gwen filled in the details in stages over the years, always referring to her special, leather-bound photo album. "The best twelve years of my life." Each time she pointed a square fingernail at a photo- rough, gardener's hands, that didn't seem to go with her beautifully made-up face and her classic perfume. "We resided in hotels, mostly, when we weren't on cruise ships. Every time we ran out of money, Saĩd would call his contact in London. A piece of jewellery would be sent. I'd wear it then we'd sell it, using the proceeds on which to live.

"Buenos Aires, and we stayed at the Governor's house..." Gwen jabbed at a lovely photo taken by a cerulean blue pool. She was wearing an amethyst tiara.

"Barbados, and we stayed at the Chancellor's home..." This time Gwen was in some kind of tropical garden, decorated in elaborate diamond and pearl earrings.

"New York, and we stayed at the Algonquin..." Gwen said, as Ruby viewed a lovely photo of a happy Gwen sitting by a bookcase, showing off a stunning sapphire necklace.

"Hong Kong, and we rented an apartment for a year..." Gwen was in an emerald choker, her earrings reaching her shoulders.

"Sydney. Before the days of the opera house..." Gwen was photographed wearing what looked like a mesh of moonstones set in a complex neck confection.

"Delhi. Then down to Kandy..." Photos of yet more diamonds and deliquescent aquamarines shone out at Ruby. She could understand why her parents might get covetous, and said so. She was not averse to finery herself, having developed a rather eclectic, teenage way of dressing.

"I'm thinking about becoming an archaeologist."

"Then you'll want to visit Egypt. I did - I insisted." Gwen pulled out another photo, and this time she was bedecked in a pearl tiara with colossal cluster earrings. "But that's when Saïd started to get ill. I've always felt guilty..." Gwen's rubbed her forehead (she seemed to flag easily these days) shooing Ruby away, and the conversation was aborted until their next meeting.

"I think it was passing up the Red Sea. He knew he could never return to Saudi Arabia. If he had his mother would have been killed, and that thought destroyed him inside. Then they had all that Suez Canal business going on, so we had to backtrack. I've stood on all six continents, you know," Gwen changed the subject. "Do your mother and father know I've definitely sold the jewellery - have you told them?"

"No." Ruby rather liked imagining them digging furiously in

the garden, like dogs seeking out a previously-secreted bone. "Good girl."

"After that we sailed down to Zanzibar. Then we moved on. We docked in Cape Town, but weren't allowed to disembark; there was an outbreak of yellow fever on-board. But the authorities did put on a boxing match for our entertainment on the Victoria and Alfred Waterfront. Then we sailed around the bulge and into Morocco. By then most of the money had run out. Saïd knew he was dying - lung cancer - he smoked those wretched Senior Service cigarettes. Not just the odd Sobranie Cocktail, like me." As if on cue, Gwen coughed and lighted one of these, positioning it in her holder. "He gave me the permissions to his safe deposit box. He died on a horrid, muggy June day, in our apartment. I had him cremated and scattered the ashes into the Strait of Gibraltar as I took passage."

Gwen showed Ruby a photo of her wearing her favourite necklace; a series of small rubies in a fantastic gold mesh, with a central star and teardrop strands hanging down. "Bloodhead, he called me. He loved the way this necklace matched me."

Ruby was incredulous. "That's what my brothers used to call me! It was meant as an insult, but I actually quite like it..."

"From Saïd's lips it was a compliment. I haven't parted with that one necklace. Of course, I made my way up through Europe, but it was such a blur. I couldn't see the countries for my teardrops. I loved him so much... I was so very numb..."

Gwen ticked them off on her fingertips; "South of France, Italy, Portugal. Even pretty Holland; one blur. I busied myself caring for my dying mama, lived with Aubrey for a while before he went to university- waste of money that was- and married Ted."

Somewhere along the line Ruby's plans changed. She still wanted to travel, but now wanted to be a cartographer. "Mum and Dad want me to work in a factory, like my brothers. And get married and have kids. But I don't want that."

"Wise choice," Gwen said.

Gwen's drinks cabinet was starting to look as faded as her, so Ruby designed a new map, which Gwen had transformed into a new globe bar. She died just before Ruby graduated. "Promise me you'll do what you have to do..." she kept reiterating in the hospice, which Ruby found odd.

Her parents were relieved when they took ownership of the cottage; glad that it hadn't gone to their whipper-snapper daughter. They set about digging up the garden, and Ruby imagined Gwen laughing at them from beyond her grave. "That garden floods - I doubt even my pets' skeletons are left!"

Ruby inherited Gwen's globe and her clothing. "haven't parted with that one necklace,'" Gwen had said, and it was right under her parents' noses. She made a decision and contacted the V&A Museum; there was going to be a small exhibition telling Gwen's story and including her personal artefacts. "Promise me you'll do what you have to do..." Ruby didn't know if she could ever part with her globe, but she did know that she now had the means to get on with her life in the way she wanted.

On Gwen's globe bar, overlooked by Ruby's teetotal parents, was her bloodhead trail, mapped out in small, red stones. The little rubies were like spots of blood flowing like pinpricks from a needle, mounted in gold and celebrating Gwen's love journey, the star centrepiece of the necklace now marking the spot where Saïd had died; the teardrops representing the remaining, broken-hearted steps home. It was all there, hidden in plain sight- the journey her parents knew nothing about as they hadn't bothered to get to know Gwen well enough to understand its significance.

On the exhibition opening evening Ruby gave her speech and viewed the globe, running her fingertips over the cold glass cabinet. She raised her red glass of gin and bitters to the heavens, smiling respectfully.

Elaine Rockett is a fiction and non-fiction writer from London who documents her domestic travels on her blog: - http://elainerockett.blogspot.com/?m=1 She has written several short stories and has published her first novel, a modern family saga entitled "The Reject's Club." She possesses an MA in Creative Writing.

CONFESSIONS OF A CLOCK-WALKER

By Lucia Kali

I was smuggled in the autumn, in the back of a cart containing apples. If anybody asked. The apples masked the trinkets pilfered on the way, and me -- wild-eyed slip of a wretch that I was -- wanted for killing a scoundrel. These weren't long after the days of burning witches, when women were suspects through simply surviving.

I was saved by the charity of thieves. The clemency of criminals. By men who knew the cost of cruelty, and the evanescence of what is right.

I had escaped my father and married young as was done in those days, to a man much older than myself. He promised me the sun, eclipsed by drunken days. But the sun really was a great ball of fire, hurtling at me with alacrity: a marriage that burnt me up inside and out.

An eight-year sentence. Served under a savage, merciless bastard.

He plucked me out so frail and fresh, as unripe flesh to pulp and maim. In his eyes I envisaged my hero, but I was no more than a piece of fruit that was rapidly rotting, with wasps and flies hustling around it. Or perhaps a waning flower, wilted and dying. Divinely and duly his, to do just as he pleased. An object of not all much value. He battered the love out of me, and then kept going: walloped us to one portentous, autumnal night. The night that changed the score.

Down by the water, decaying leaves swept our feet and boats belched out the rich whiff of coal. His hands around my neck, breathless crushing bricks beneath the bridge. His sonorous growl, a growing echo. Done for, done for now.

Did anyone see us? A gentleman, but he crossed the street. Then tiptoed, hushing his cane to silence its tap.

The strife of the masses? Oh, how distasteful.

My husband used my bonnet to drag me down the stony steps to the canal. There was a finality to him that was usually lacking and I knew my time was up. This was really it -- twenty-four years of toil, ending... just as you'd expect, I s'pose. The sad end of a sad life. The deed would be done and this is where I'd be discarded.

Except that as he throttled on, something else happened.

Turns out a couple of likely lads were looking on. I'd never known anyone to step in until this point and for a few years in my naivety, I believed they were angels. The habit of religion is a hard one to give up.

I take a break to cherish it. The sublime series of events. Astonishing pressure, my windpipe caving in, a crushing need for air. The tunnel is closing in, goodnight. But I'm coughing as I'm gulping down air and, what? Am I dead? He'd fallen away, knocked down by heaven. If heaven was a hammer. But what did I know as I caught back my breath? I was relieved he'd changed his mind. Still beneath the bridge, gasping and grappling, unaware I'd been reborn. I didn't know until later that there was a weighted sack by the lock, waiting for a victim. So his trick had been reversed; a nasty curse thrown back upon him. Do unto others as they'll have done to you.

They were thieves by trade, and heroes by nature. They understood the squalid sentiments of men.

We left that night, leaving for The City of Musing Screws. They sang a rhyme to lull my misgivings.

The City of Musing Screws

Where fortune's fair and fine

Cos the tutors all drink wine

& in their pockets we will find

The answers

Are all mine

Until daylight broke and the roads clogged with men of business and travel, when the words were changed.

I was alive!

Alive, more alive than I had ever been or would ever be again.

Awakened, wild, apples in my eye and feathers in my cap.
Transcending but cautious, close to the edge.

Rocking up and wary, I stuck close to my heroes' tattered wings. There were favours to forge. Flavours to fashion. An exorcism, an establishing and excess to excel at. The oldest professions and means to the end.

I got set up rather nicely. The dirty work got bleached. I stumbled upon clock-walking and the city's hidden route. I was working, walking my patch, when I found it. Changed the game again. If you don't know, it goes like this: each lap is a rotation of the clock by one year. Clock-walking, the living legend. Clock-walking as the longer form of hell. Time to be mastered for the feet of a chosen few.

I walked off ten years in the first evening.

The route can't be uttered but its life is allusions. I am sure it revels in blood.

I reversed that cut-throat marriage. Thus my options and prospects increased.

Dramatically. It was like buying back innocence. I was doing alright but a woman back then was as good as dead without a man. Her vocation lay in who she wed. I'd already buggered up on my first one, even if it wasn't my fault. But the law-abiding, God-fearing, scratching-their-backside masses did not see it like that. For those lot, no matter what way you painted, I was a fallen woman. With my found family of rogues.

One lap, one year. Ten laps and -- Lose ten years and you become a different person. A better person: better fed in better circumstances with a better chance to thrive.

My veiled history did hinder my mission, and rejecting my hero's proposal was done with a heavy heart.

It took longer than I will write here for there were many favours I still had to make, and much erasing of said favours. I learned to read and to write. My innocence was a hard-earned performance, an agonising dance of deceit that soared in its deliverance as I shrank and smirked inside. There is no honour among privilege.

I got my gold ticket, eventually. He was a lover of progress, a well-established writer. The keeper of a little chunk of my withered, worn-out soul. A gentle, genuine man. A gentleman, unequivocally. Not in euphemism for an incorrigible maggot ('well-bred', 'well-dressed' or well not).

He taught me everything. Refined me like wine as we gulped back lots of it. The days were luxurious. We langoured in literature and culture.

When he died, that whole life caved in with his casket: an ornate, elaborate affair. We were together for twenty years. Ostensibly, I was 'eighteen' when we married. In truth my days more closely numbered his.

I'll admit his death elicited some relief. My eternal youth was becoming incredible, even to my love. While he teased that I enchanted him, I did not want this seed of sorcery to bud and flower. Ineluctably, it did, amidst his remaining family. His rotten sisters, their rotten children and the rotten children's children after them.

Gladys. Gladless. The only name I'll mention. A dragon by any other. The host of most of the inciting antipathy. The only beast who could invoke a witch hunt in the 19th C. during the height of the spiritualist movement.

The prosecution maintained that I had bewitched her brother. It was slander, what they said. How they belittled his intellect. Accused him of being 'soft', 'weak-minded' and 'infirm'.

'The kind of man who is an artist and therefore prey to this kind of thing.'

The tables had tipped and the jury ruled in favour of injustice. My only saving grace lay in the sagacity and understanding of the judge, who took pity on the plainness and simplicity of the jurors and most crucially -- on me, the victim of this witch hunt. An 'evil enchantress', a 'sourceless sorceress', or a 'siren for up-standing men'. (Many circles included the judge in this).

What catalysed the trial and stirred the minds of the public was a forty-year-old statement. It had been dredged via another police force in a completely different area by my enemy's excellent lawyer and a distant relation or other of Gladless'. My hubby's sister was ruthless and impassioned in her insistence that I would not receive a shred of her family's fortune. Her fervour and zeal was so white-hot, that she would zestfully support my execution.

In another town, forty years ago, a gentleman had witnessed a disagreement between a man and his woman. They were 'of a low class' and fearing his safety he had scuttled on, 'gratefully unnoticed'. But as he recalled the 'fragility of the girl' and the 'brute strength of the man', his conscience had bothered him (so gentlemen could feel?) and he'd found a policeman. Maybe an hour later, they had descended down the towpath where the girl had been dragged.

There was blood at the scene and the lock was emptied. They found a body. Freshly dead, his head smashed in. They could only conclude she had found some 'feminine, frenzied strength' and overturned the man. The gentleman who'd begun this matter then decided that in his 'terror and fear' he must have misremembered this mystery woman. Her pleas could have been no more than decoys. She was obviously less fragile than he had felt. Perhaps she had manipulated him? The gentleman was congratulated on his strength of mind and character. A lesser man may have followed her.

The mystery woman was never caught, although the man (and subsequently the woman) was identified.

As was habit among ladies at the time, upon hearing this I fainted.

I remembered that gentleman, rushing off on that misty night. Did they mean to say he had tried to help me? And now his assistance would break my neck, belatedly?

Her lawyer was good. Gladless' hate had inspired the people. It would seem my time was up.

Let us take a moment to salute the skills of science. Their power to have saved my neck and the glimmer of providence that they shimmered down.

The prosecution was stunning in their delivery of a debauched and dissolute defendant, who could manipulate time as she mashed men's skulls. But the judge wouldn't have it. There would be nothing so 'contravened against science' upheld in his court.

I was a sixty-four-year-old woman in the body of a twenty-year-old, passing off as thirty-eight. My existence contravened science.

And the jury thought so too.

Yet thanks to the judge I did not hang. Instead they sentenced me to twenty years imprisonment, subject to the 'evidential ageing of my mortal body'.

In those lonely walls, away from my walks, I slowly declined. We could not speak but were made to dwell on our wrongs. But our minds were stuck, caught and re-living the wrongs which had been done to us. The ever-present cold and damp, the cellar-like chill, recaptured my early years and penetrated the rags of my soul. It made me severe. Their tricks turned me glacial.

But indurate and unyielding, they let me out.

Their mistake, they should've killed me. Rather than leave the hate to crystallise. A diamond of repulsion beneath my reduced body, hidden behind my toothless acquiescence. Another cross to bear.

I leave and I mine it out of myself. I toss out that old shape and hair.

The battered little bitch was long thrown on the heap. Out of her ashes rose ruthlessness and reprisals.

I made my own cash in the only way they would let me. But I glow in the shadows. I dazzle up the night.

It is mine. I am your nightmares. I merge with the times. I take out their eyes,

Then I eat them. It is banal and expected, just like us all.

My empire balloons around me. Inflates up any strip and tips up many wallets.

I am fed by your revulsion. It propels me through my walks. I am vaginal teeth and gun-toting nuns.

Lucia Kali is a part-time writer who lives in Oxford, UK. She is inspired to write by life and because she feels the need to. She writes because the words are demanding to come out.

SOCIAL SHADE

By James Dwyer

People often mistake my shade of navy as blue. They'll ask what's wrong, wonder why I'm uncomfortable, or believe that I'm sad. But that's just their colour distorting mine. Left to myself, my shade of navy is quite content. It's often satisfied, if seldom proud. In extreme cases, if someone is orange with interest or an unrelated excitement, it can brighten my navy to cyan. The misinterpretation of this lighter blue is worse. Mistaken for sulking or self-pity, I'll be told to cheer up. Cyan is also the shade of loneliness, yet it's rarely seen. Maybe it prefers its own company.

When people comment on my colour, it's much easier for me to shift my darker blue to black, to signal my annoyance, and ready myself for rage. It rarely comes to that. The passing interest between other people's shades and mine are just that. They pass. They flicker and they flit like so many shades I see. Some people can pulse between ten different colours in the same number of seconds. Mine generally stays the same.

My brother is coming to stay with me tomorrow. He's in town for a week of training with his work and I foolishly said yes when he asked if he could crash with me. And crash is the word. Like someone asking to park their car in your living room instead of your drive. His life is so loud. Mine is quiet. His energy is random and fierce. I keep mine more controlled.

I prefer a thermostat to throwing logs. It means I don't have to worry about smoke, or sparks, or burning out.

But I still said yes. Even in our new world where emotions are broadcast so vividly, enough to paint our surroundings with a bubble of bright colour, I still can't be honest with my brother. How can you tell someone who loves you that you don't enjoy spending time with them? That you love them, but you prefer to hold that love at a distance. To enjoy it through photographs or messages or even memory – if only there was a way we could relive life's events without having to live through them first.

When I get home from work, I collapse in my reading chair. Sometimes my shade of content navy will change to the light orange of anticipation or the dull gold of calm. Sparkles of joy can light up my colour while I'm vacationing inside my book. Now, however, as I prepare for the best part of my day, the room is the yellow of sick anxiety, thinking about tomorrow when my brother comes to stay. It takes time to return my world to navy, the shade a little light so even I begin to wonder if this might not be despair. But, within the hour, as I finish my book, the room's colour blossoms with the solid depth of cerulean satisfaction. I stare at the cover in fondness, my eyes appreciating small details afresh. My fingers brush through the pages, as if cherished memory was something I could physically touch. I don't want to let go.

Before, I made the mistake of trying to share this satisfaction. For such an endless ocean that could swell with proud azure, I find the internet is mostly mired brown with discontent.

People confuse criticisms with critiques. They mistake impassioned interest with polarised opinion. They fill up an infinite space with polluted ramblings, words so over-blown they become distended and unrecognisable to read. Too much is said or too little, needlessly negative or oblivious with bliss. I suppose the power to broadcast needs to be fuelled by some extreme. No place for a few words more moderately spoken, or if there is then I'll never find it buried beneath all those loud demands for social attention.

The next day at work I'm apprehensive, a rotting lemon as my shade. My colleagues express their usual orange interest in my colour. Some even see this change as positive and force out the patronising gold of joy. Their intrusive moods distort my colour, once again confusing it with their own. I'm disgusted by their falseness, leaving each situation before I turn my surroundings green. Better to leave people white with confusion than reveal to them what I truly think. Or is that being false as well? Maybe I'm just rude. Do I even know why other people bother me so much? You'd think that this constant projection of our emotional colour would lead to a better understanding of them. Or do we simply get dazzled by the lights.

Peter arrives later than he said he would. He's exhausted and sweating from the drive. After dumping his bags on my floor, he collapses in a chair and kicks off his socks and shoes. He fills the room with complaints about being tired, and lists all the thorns and nettles in his life. His shade isn't the black of irritation though. He's gold from the joy of companionship and sharing. I don't think I'll ever understand that, but for once I'm glad of his intruding shade. It makes the blue of my discomfort easier to hide.

I offer sympathetic noises back at him to be polite. When he's run out of dramatic conflicts he's overcome, my brother begins to throw random statements at me that are too awkward for me to catch. Even if I'm able to get a grasp on one or two, they'll swiftly clatter shapeless to the floor. I never hold any long enough to create a conversation from it. The blue of my discomfort begins to turn red with embarrassment. I even see a few grey slashes of shame. My brother and I had been best friends when we were kids. We made efforts for our paths not to drift apart too much, but I realise now that somewhere along that road my efforts had completely stopped. Here was Peter doing his best to enjoy our time together, and here I was waiting for it to be done.

Noticing my change in shade, Peter smiles at me and says it's probably time he went to bed. His colour doesn't go black, or brown, or green at my antisocial display. My brother's shade goes silver before he says goodnight. Silver, the colour of acceptance. I can't remember the last time I've seen that.

I spend all of the next day blazing teal with determination. I prepare topics of conversation in my head with which I know we share an interest, ones where both of us will be able to contribute with genuine energy. I'm so ready when I get home that the purple of my disappointment hits me like a solid wall when I find my brother isn't there. His training must have gone on late. Or maybe he met people he knew there from work and was spending his time with them instead. Which was fine. Completely normal behaviour, really. A situation that best suited us both.

Not knowing when Peter would be back, I settle in for my evening read like I always do. It doesn't take long for the shade of purple pulsing through the room to descend back down to navy. I'd never considered contentment to be a dissension from disappointment before, but my dark blue surroundings seem to press in on me with weight. Instead of escaping deep inside my new book as I always would, my mind wanders anywhere else. I think about the fun my brother must be having with anyone but me. I fantasise about joining them, pretending that I wouldn't drag the collective mood down. But more than anything, my mind thinks about the control I claim when I insist that I'm holding onto my shade of dark blue. This new weight that my navy has gained lets me see how unsteady my grip actually is. I can see it slip. Or has it already happened? Long ago, without my notice, could my shade have dropped and I sink down with it, pretending that my grasp has never changed.

Is that the benefit of other people? A consensus to show what an individual might not let himself see? And there I thought that other people were just beasts of habit. Dogs barking at each other without meaning, racing around chasing sticks. They wag their tails at every unremarkable event, and pant with excitement at the same things every day. Was happiness worth that price? Would I rather sit apart and sneer at them like a cat? Alone in my home, not reading my book, I suddenly laugh. I imagine myself sharing these thoughts with

Peter and I picture his response. Maybe you should get a pet, he'd say. And maybe he'd be right.

When Peter comes back, he's delightfully drunk. Most of that delight is his, but his golden joy is so bright, tinted pink with giddiness, that I'm transformed against my will. He bursts into the funniest stories of his night and I smile back at him with real comradery. I even laugh along with the good times he's had before suddenly his smile runs fleeing from my home. There's too many shades fracturing throughout the room for me to understand what's happening. Goodnight Denis, he says then, I love you, brother. I mumble something back, but remain in my seat as he trudges up to bed. I sit there, in my reading chair, with my book still held open, paused in mid-read, and I wonder what went wrong.

The following morning I'm on a day-off from work. Peter's up and out before I wake. I feel guilty that I missed him. The grey remains with me for the day, colouring my entire house, even following me outside when I try to read my book in the sun. The neighbours who walk past tut and shake their heads at me for bringing such dullness out in public. The golden brilliance of their enjoyment – of the sun, of the heat, of the exhilaration they feel being part of it – all adds to their surroundings. My struggling shades only ever take away. Falling deeper down that spiral, I retreat back inside.

I find haven in my newest book, which has finally consumed me. The characters have revealed themselves to be people I'd like to know. They are living interesting lives in places where I would love to be. They are solving small mysteries and overcoming dramatic conflict and I am brought to tears that they are allowing me to be part of it. It's amazing what a little distance can do to bring my heart closer. The simple control of holding a page in my hand and I can surrender myself to it completely.

I'm torn away from that reality by the vibration of my phone. It's Peter. He's messaged me to say, good news! Training's been cancelled. The instructor got called away. They're going to finish everything remotely. It means he'll be back in a minute to pick up his things and let me return to my peace.

I don't know how to feel. I should be happy, I suppose, but my world has turned into a blur of colour that I can no longer see. Stare at something too long and your eyes lose focus. Think about something too much and all meaning becomes lost.

Peter thumps back to my home with his usual energy. The awkwardness and self-reflection from before are nowhere to be seen. He once more fills the air with statements, although this time spiced with questions. It forces my mind to move along with him at the same speed. I'm getting caught up in his shade again, but I'm grateful for it because it pulls me out from my own. Before I know it, I'm asking if he'd like to do something together next weekend. His surprise is brief and blinding, an overture to his smile. Then it's my turn to colour white as he asks if he can borrow some books.

My books. My most precious possessions. The only joy in my days. And yet I'm somehow filled with more happiness now to be giving these treasures away. I add my knowledge of these novels to my experience of my brother, and I recommend the ones that he would hopefully like best. I try to give him five of my favourites, but he holds up his hand at three.

As soon as I finish these, he says, I'll come back again to get some more.

Okay, I say, you can come back any time. But message me once you've finished them. I'd love to know how they make you feel.

James lives in East Cork, Ireland. A writer by day and martial arts instructor by night, he writes fantasy novels with Paused Books but loves short stories of every genre.

CAROLINA

By Leslie Roberts

The eucalyptus stood tall and magnificent against the early evening sun. Paul wondered if his and Carolina's initials were still visible on its flaking trunk, but he couldn't get near it in this traffic. What had once been a quiet alleyway was now a thoroughfare. He marvelled that the tree had thrived among the fumes. He remembered laughter, stolen kisses, whispered oaths beneath those branches. The prospect of seeing her again both terrified and excited him.

A honking scooter weaved close by. He moved on. The whitewashed church seemed smaller now, diminished by the urban sprawl which merged the once-secluded village with the neighbouring town.

The house, though unchanged, was now sandwiched between a petrol station and a fast-food restaurant. He approached the door, fearing yet hoping the house might be abandoned. Movement at a downstairs window quickened his heart. He knocked at the door before he could change his mind.

It took him several seconds to recognise the plump, middle aged man who answered. Only gradually did the azure eyes and the uneven cast of the mouth conjure up the image of Raphael's younger, more athletic self.

"Yes? What can I do for you?"

Paul smiled at the melodious Asturias accent, once so familiar.

"I'm sorry to disturb…," Paul began, conscious how much his own spoken Spanish had changed, "I was passing through, and… Do you remember me, Raphael?"

As Raphael grappled with his thoughts, a shrill voice, laden with anxiety, came from the gloom behind him.

"Who is it, Raphael?"

Raphael, turned his head without taking his eyes from Paul. "It's nothing. Just a friend from the stables." He leaned towards Paul and whispered, "Don't let her know who you are. She won't recognise you. I'll explain."

A white-haired lady hobbled into view. Paul gasped to see how the years had ravaged Carolina's mother. Her pale, emaciated face hung unevenly as though she had suffered a stroke. She wheezed from the effort of walking, and relied heavily on her stick.

"Who is it?" The woman glared at Paul as if he were attempting a break-in.

Raphael took her by the shoulders and whispered, as though to a small child. "It's alright. It's a friend from the stables." He steered the old lady inside, limping badly himself. He beckoned for Paul to follow.

Paul studied the sitting room. Bare walls, stone floor, woven carpet, rattan chairs, all the same. Only the colour TV, large and blinking, conceded to modernity. Raphael sat his mother-in-law in front of the screen and turned up the volume. Instantly, she was absorbed by some quiz game which Paul recognised but had never properly watched. Raphael ushered him into another room, where they spoke in hushed tones.

"She's not well." Raphael described tiny circles at his temple with an index finger. "Her mind…"

"I'm sorry, "said Paul, shuffling his feet, "she was such a lively lady."

Raphael shrugged, adopted a smile. "Just look at you! Hardly a boy when you left, now you're a respectable businessman. Smart suit. And your Spanish is so fluent."

"I live in Columbia now," said Paul. "After the hospitality I enjoyed here I could never live in England." They both laughed.

"It's good to see you again. What a surprise!" Raphael took two glasses from a cupboard and poured amber liquid from a frosted glass bottle. They clinked tumblers and drank to each other's health. Paul strained for sounds beyond the door, but heard only applause from the TV.

Raphael tweaked Paul's lapel. "What are you doing now, to buy such expensive suits?"

"Nothing terribly exciting. I offer legal advice to Brits living in Bogotá. You know the sort; they like the better climate but can't be bothered to learn the language. How about you? Still with the riding school?" Raphael looked down. "Strictly administration. I shattered my leg in a fall and it ended my riding career."

"My God! I had no idea. I'm so sorry."

Raphael shrugged. "Things have been tough, one way and another, but life goes on." He stared. "Didn't you receive my letters?"

"Letters? No." Paul stared at his feet. "And I hardly wrote myself. I'm sorry." After a short pause, he asked. "How did it happen?"

Raphael swallowed, batting the air as though swatting a fly. "It doesn't matter, now. Tell me about yourself."

Paul brought him up to date with his life since university. They reminisced about their shared adventures, when Paul, studying Spanish, lived in a nearby pension.

"How about that day we went to Toledo," said Raphael, "and my old banger broke down?"

Surprised that Raphael remembered the occasion with such fondness, Paul himself recalled the harsh wine, the scorching sun, and his walk by the river with Carolina. "Toledo. So beautiful!"

"Hmm! Less so when you're stuck for hours in a garage!" Raphael replied.

"How's Carolina?" Paul kept the question as casual as

possible. Raphael's face froze into a painful mask of embarrassment. "Paul... My letters. I always wondered why you didn't reply. He fixed the tiled floor with a cold gaze and almost choked. "Carolina died."

A long, imponderable silence descended as the men struggled, one to conquer his grief, the other to comprehend the enormity of what he had heard.

"Died?" Paul's stomach heaved. His mouth dried. "It can't be. How? When?"

Raphael ran a palm over his forehead. The words came out with difficulty. "We never found out why. They say she killed herself, but I've never believed it." Tears filled his deep blue eyes.

"Suicide? No, surely..." Paul stuttered. "Why? How?"

"It happened about four months after you left. She was found hanging from that big eucalyptus by the main road, early one morning. Raphael leaned heavily against the wall. Shook his head. "A complete mystery."

Paul could hardly breathe. He struggled for words, but mumbled, "Raphael, I'm, I'm so... I had no idea."

The two men embraced, absorbing each other's grief. Embarrassment separated them.

Raphael wiped his eyes. "I'm sorry you had to hear about it like this, Paul. I can't believe... my letters."

They shared a moment's silence before Raphael took a deep breath. "All such a long time ago, now." He forced a smile. "Life goes on."

"Where's my supper?" The old woman's voice resonated from the other room. Raphael grimaced in mock anger, shrugged in resignation, and stood. "See what I mean? Life goes on."

"Sorry," Paul said, "it's an awkward time. I should have phoned first."

Did they even have a telephone? Looking around, he saw a photograph he had taken of Carolina that afternoon in Toledo; dark, windswept hair and eyes alive with happiness. The memories flooded back.

They had left Raphael at the garage and strolled along the river bank to picnic in the woods. Parched from the heat, the spiced chorizo and dry bread, they found a café where they drank water and shared a bottle of house red. They raced each other back towards the river and into the shade of the trees.

Raphael's voice interrupted his memories. "You will eat with us, of course."

"Oh no, really, Raphael, I won't put you out."

"You are putting no-one out," the Spaniard retorted, already tossing salad in a huge porcelain bowl. "I have learned to cook since being alone." He began beating eggs in a smaller bowl. Paul watched the quivering flesh beneath his chin as he whisked the eggs to a deep, yellow froth.

They had slept, he and Carolina, entwined in each other's arms, among the hibiscus and jasmine. Afterwards, she was consumed with remorse and spoke of sin and atonement. She protested that she was married, insisted she loved her husband.

"It must never happen again," she said, brushing the leaves from her skirt and adjusting her top. Paul kissed her bare arm, and she lashed out, accusing him of being the devil come to tempt her.

Paul laughed. "You are even more beautiful when angry."

"Seventy-five and still eating like a horse," Raphael said, adding garnish to the salad.

"Sorry? What?"

"Mamma." She eats like a bloody horse. Come on, bring yours in. Mustn't keep her waiting." He led the way into the dining room and placed an omelette before the old woman, already sitting. He fetched a carafe of wine.

Paul had forgotten about the prayers. He clasped his fingers as Raphael said Grace. As they ate, they spoke briefly of Paul's life in Bogotá, and of Raphael's attempts to survive on the business the stables brought in. When the conversation drifted back to Carolina, Raphael gave an urgent, almost imperceptible shake of his head and changed the subject.

They finished the meal in almost complete silence. From where he sat, Paul observed a photograph of Carolina in happier times, laughter lines radiating from the corners of her eyes. He recalled kissing tears from those eyes. After Toledo, as soon as the opportunity had arisen, she had again succumbed.

"I am so weak," she railed, and revealed an unsuspected degree of piety: "I deserve to go to hell."

When Raphael toured with his riding team, winning medals throughout Europe that year, Paul had visited her most nights, stealing into the house after midnight, leaving before dawn.

Carolina's mother cast suspicious glances at Paul as they ate. Finally, she stared hard and asked: "Have we met before, young man?"

Raphael answered: "He visited once, Mamma. Long ago."

She returned to her TV while the men took the dishes to the kitchen. Raphael washed, Paul dried.

"She becomes distraught when Carolina's name is mentioned. It's what sent her crazy, you know. Raphael stopped washing and stared ahead at nothing in particular. "It is a terrible thing to lose one's child." Tears welled as he spoke.

They sat at the kitchen table, each in the privacy of his own thoughts. Paul closed his eyes and remembered Carolina once more, sleeping peacefully in dappled sunlight.

She had become more accepting of her weakness. "I wish we could be together like this always," she had said. The early sun streamed through the shutters, striations of light and shade across her face and breasts. They made love once more, and by the time he threw on his clothes it was way past the time he had vowed to leave. He snatched a final kiss while pulling on a boot.

On the landing, he met Carolina's mother, a proud Castilian widow who held herself erect. They stared at each other without speaking before he fled.

Paul and Raphael sat together. Occasional platitudes punctuated the silence. The church bell sounded for Vespers.

"I should be going." Paul rose awkwardly.

At the door, the two men embraced again. The light from the fast-food restaurant highlighted Raphael's tears.

"Sorry," Raphael said. "Seeing you again has brought it all back. Such happy times." He wiped his face with an open hand, "I get like this when I think how things might have been."

Paul would not trust himself to speak, but placed a hand on the Spaniard's shoulder. He was about to turn away when Raphael added, "They found she was carrying my baby, you know."

Paul, open-mouthed, again took the Spaniard into his arms, relieved to conceal his own expression. He felt Raphael's gentle sobbing. "Sorry," he whispered, then turned abruptly and marched down the driveway toward the street.

Raphael shouted, "Keep in touch."

Paul glanced only briefly at the menacing silhouette of the eucalyptus, its accusing limbs outstretched against a shimmering moon.

Leslie has had several short stories published. His Justice and Other Short Stories is available through Amazon. Leslie lives with his wife in Cornwall in the UK where, between gardening, DIY and coastal walks, he is putting the final touches to a fictional memoir of Sophie Dawes (1790-1840).

THE UNQUIET GRAVE

By Becca Brown

Samson's twin hills were virtually obscured by driving rain and darkness. On the farther hill to the right, the light from Teän's family's hearth was almost invisible, and the Webber family's fire was blotted out on the mound directly behind her. The stretch of sand beneath Teän's feet had turned inky, lit only by spattered moonlight that stretched into a broiling sea. She had come out, as she did every evening, to scan the horizon for her brother's boat. Usually, even on a drizzly night, she could see the shores of the other inhabited islands from anywhere on Samson's barren hills. Or at the very least, Bishop Rock lighthouse's beam on the Western Rocks were visible, surrounded by the souls of drowned sailors. Tonight, there was little beyond the darkness. As she moved down the bay, her lips moved in quiet song. It might have been a song her mother had taught her, or perhaps her grandmother. She couldn't remember. The lyrics were whipped away by the wind as soon as they'd left her mouth, snatched back into the ether by an affronted wind-nymph.

Cold blows the wind of night, sweet-heart,

Cold are the drops of rain;

The very first love that ever I had,

In green-wood he was slain.

Her eyes strained as she eyed the beach before her. Tëan's family's little skip lay somewhere to her left, useless amongst waves as large as these. Not that I'd get in it anyway, she thought. Out to sea a shape caught her eye amongst the darkness., The Bonnet, a lifeboat gig crammed with crew called to rescue stranded sailors. She blinked. It disappeared. It was probably her imagination, or a ghost. She said a silent prayer for them either way. The real pilot gigs always steered clear of Samson.

Teän could understand why her neighbours avoided her island. She must look mad, barefoot and unafraid, out in a storm that would take hundreds of lives in its course. In the past, Samson had boasted a small but hardy community. Only her family and the Webbers remained, now. Even they were slowly starving, on a weak diet of potatoes and limpets and occasional honey extracted from heather from the headland. The people of the Isles had always been tough, but with that toughness came incessant self-preservation; charity on neighbouring St Mary's did not extend to helping the two mad families on a dying island. Teän had never explicitly heard islanders call her homeland cursed, but she felt it in the way they inched away from her every time she had taken a trip to the St Mary's store as a child, or tutted at her bare feet and bones jutting through her smock. No-one thought to give her a meal. If they're mad enough to exile themselves, let them, they muttered after her.

She did understand people's misgivings. If you weren't familiar with Samson's ghouls like she was, it could appear quite unsavoury. You had to be born here to be truly comfortable. Souls were everywhere, wandering the barren hills. Graves and ancient burial sites of Teän's ancestors littered the hills, and the bay seemed to lure wrecks to her shores. Just five years ago, a plagued ship's crew had been released from the Pest House on St Helen's a week early and one lad had taken a merry day trip to Samson, shacked up with a girl of a third family, and within a month they had all died in their home, covered in buboes. Even then, her family stayed.

Last summer, her brother had not returned from a trip with friends that was only supposed to last a week - he'd been gone three months, or thereabouts. Even then, they'd stayed. The rest of the family would die here by choice, but Teän's fate was worse, or so she reckoned. It had been years since she had left Samson at all, and likely she never would again. Above all else, Tëan loathed deep water - and it had transformed her family home into a prison. The ocean roared before her now, writhing like an animal in pain. It seemed to sense her fear and multiply it tenfold. Taunting her. She tried to focus on the song, rather than the growing swell.

Cold are my lips in death, sweet-heart,

My breath is earthy strong...

Her father, William Woodcock Jr., was the last of his 5 siblings stubbornly clinging, like the limpets he survived on, to his beloved island. He was known on Bryher as 'Mad Ole Will', but everyone on Scilly knew it was a fine line between insanity and instinct - and nobody could deny his gut. Teän's mother Judith - originally of the neighbouring Webber family - had blanched when William had brought back the corpse of their family dog for dinner in the winter of 1851. But they'd cooked and eaten it diligently, knowing their father hadn't survived 50 years on the island by being sentimental. As usual, he was right. It was the only thing they ate that week. The icy storms had made venturing outside impossible, and they became very grateful for dear old Rex's sacrifice. Teän didn't think Rex blamed her. He still sat at her feet during dinner sometimes, as he had done when he was alive. She was only sorry to miss his body heat warming her chilblained toes - he was cold through now, and glowed softly.

...if you do touch my clay-cold lips,

Your time will not be long.

From the size of the storm whipping up around Teän on this particular night, she suspected this winter would be another challenging one. She knelt in the silt and plucked up a few razor clams, jutting out of the sand like they were gasping for air. Tëan hated clams, but she hated the familiar growl of her stomach more. Her eyes, after so many years on an island with no lamps, were accustomed to the night, so gathering in darkness as she scanned the horizon was no bother. But even she still saw ghostly mirages, out to sea: a galleon filled with skeletal crew; a flailing limb in the water; a body thwacking against the gallows on Hangman's Island to her left, where Admiral Blake had strung up his crew two centuries ago. Her mother, bless her soul, tried to tell her that her fear of the deep water was an instinct instilled by her drowned ancestors, but the ghosts she saw at sea did not feel rational. They were lost souls, untethered and sad. She hoped so very dearly that her brother was not one of them. She dusted herself of wet sand, picked up her basket full of samphire and clams, turned her back and headed for home on the adjacent hill.

What is it that you want of me,

And will not let me sleep?

Your salten tears they trickle down

My winding sheet to steep.

The ghosts that greeted her on the headland were a welcome sight by comparison. Teän picked her way up a little path cut into the headland, ankles brushing through gorse that snagged at her skin. Perhaps this is why the St Mary's residents are so afraid, she wondered. They've never seen our land spirits. Only the horrible wailing ocean ones. These ghouls were hardy, steadfast, unchanging. The smell of heather wafted in the wind, bringing a honey-sweet scent. The spirits' pale light lit her way home. A viking wrapped her in their furs, even though she could not feel it. His charred face beamed down at her. They had been here the longest. They were most comfortable in their ethereal state. Near the gravestones, gaunt little William le Pour, the old island coroner, silently fussed about beside her. Her late grandparents busied themselves in the family garden as she passed, carrying kelp baskets, misty and white in hue. They were more recent, and less at ease than the vikings, but still these were not like the lost shipwrecked souls. These ghosts were her history, her surroundings, and they made her feel at home.

The hearth had gone out when Teän reached the little granite house. It was quiet, except for the soft snoring of her mother and father and siblings, congested with cold. She knelt before the grate, and a soft, cold light brushed past her. She nudged it gently, assuming it to be Rex's little spirit like usual. The little collie's ghost often appeared on winter's nights, protecting the family as he had in life. The fire took, and a soft whoosh flew up the chimney and met the cold air. She was surprised by how light the room was. The coal was limited - the luxury of wood on the island having long since gone - so the fire barely lit the room usually. Perhaps Rex's spirit was stronger than usual tonight.

She stood, and turned to store away her goods. Her eyes flickered to the table in the corner of the room, but there was no dog seated beneath the table. The light was much brighter than Rex's - she was bathed in it, cool, pulsating. She straightened, and took a deep breath. Seated at the table was the figure of a young boy. His hair was familiar, black and wavy like her own. Normally, his hair would be tousled by the wind; now, it floated above his head as though suspended in invisible water. His face looked almost startled, eyes roving around the familiar space, taking in the home he had been absent from for months. Teän had seen ghosts appear before, for the first time, but never someone she had known so well as her brother. It pained her to see the panic of his passing still in his eyes, guessing at the pain he had felt as his lungs filled with water. She wondered what had happened to him in the unaccounted months, that he'd only just been lost to the sea tonight. He would never be able to tell her.

At least he had come home, she thought. She wouldn't go and scour the horizon each evening anymore. She was glad his soul had returned home, for her mother's sake. If it hadn't, it would have gone unspoken that his ghost would be left drifting in the ocean, joining the chorus of wails of unmoored sailors begging for land. Tomorrow, when he was more at peace, perhaps he would let her lead him silently out into the garden to help their grandparents in their moonlit garden. Or perhaps play with Rex for a time. Or perhaps this is how he would stay, frozen at the table. It would make for challenging family dinners.

She stepped towards her brother, gently so as not to startle him. Her feet made no sound on the dirt floor. She eased herself into the rickety chair opposite him. His eyes flitted back and forth, and his mouth moved agape. It always took a while for death to wear off, she knew that much. Tentatively, she reached a hand out to cover his. Her hand slipped straight through his, but she stayed there anyway. His face did not change, but his eyes flickered toward her. I shall miss you, brother. As soon as he had been gone a day longer than planned, she knew he was gone. It was the way of the sea. It had been foolish, wishful thinking to stand and watch for him each day. Perhaps the other islanders were right. Samson's the cursed isle, everyone knows that. She had felt it when her brother left. She felt it every time she steered the skipper out of the shallows. She looked at her brother's tormented face. In a way, it was a comfort. She would live her life upon this barren island, shunned by society, and when she died she would become one with its folklore like her ancestors before her. She would die, anonymous and unknown, lost to fairytales and talks of curses that shrouded Samson's shores.

And well for you that bramble-leaf

Betwixt our lips was flung.

The living to the living hold,

Dead to the dead belong.

Becca is from Hertfordshire in the UK and her inspiration mostly comes from folklore - specifically English folklore - and the timeless way stories have been preserved through music. In this story she wanted to rework a classic tale of mourning a loved one.

BAD CHOICES

By Philip Gibson

Mari Patel studies her reflection suspiciously, rereads the instruction on the back of the box of Sparkle Hair Dye and cringes as she glances at her reflection again. How, what, why? The interview is in two hours in the middle of town. She really needs to get this job. What can she do? Wing it!

****

"I'm passionate about the environment," Mari says, leaning forward slightly as she perches on the front half of the interview seat. "Yeah, that's all good," the interviewer replies with a lisp. "But you know we sell fast-food, right?"

"Yeah. I was trying to explain my hair, you know, why it's, kind of… green." Mari mutters. She senses she has made a mistake but isn't quite sure what it was.

The interviewer leans back and gazes at her for a second, then exhales loudly and looks down at a document on his work desk. He picks up his partially chewed biro and starts to write on the form. His heavily tattooed arms contrast against his black tee shirt. The pen doesn't work so he stares at it and licks the point. His stainless-steel tongue piercing clicks against the nib.

"So, when can you start?" he asks.

Dean Lancaster sprawls beside Mari in his never knowingly 'made' grubby double bed. He dives to the side to grab his abandoned jeans and slides a pack of cigarettes from the front pocket. He returns to an upright position and places his back against the wall. He removes a slightly bent cigarette and a lighter from the packet.

"You want one?" he points the crumpled packet in her direction.

"Nah," she replies sleepily. "I'm awright."

"When you start babe?"

"Tonight," she wriggles towards him and looks adoringly up into his face. "I did what you asked."

"Yeah, yeah. Cool. Are you gonna change that hair or what? You look like you've gone mouldy!"

Dean lights a cigarette and sends a stream of smoke up into the heavily yellowed ceiling. Then he leans over the side of the bed to seize his jeans again and delves into the other pocket.

"Here take these. I'll bell you later. Just make sure you answer. You get me?"

Mari takes the cheap mobile from him and stashes it into her own front pocket and holds the plastic zippy up to the window so she can get a good look at the rocks. She snatches the cigarette out of his hand, places it between her lips and takes a deep inhale. Then she snakes her hand around the back of his neck, pulls him down towards her and snogs him roughly. Tobacco smoke escapes their joined mouths and circles around their heads.

"You better make sure he doesn't find out," Mari hisses.

****

The unwashed metallic grey Mercedes slides into Boyd Drive. This is a short residential road with the benefit of free parking. Both sides of the road are bordered by three-story tenement buildings, separated into ten blocks, each containing six apartments with a shared entry, closes, stairs and external front door. The steroid-enhanced driver turns to his almost identical navigator and raises an eyebrow. In the rear seat Wee-G grasps a roll of wide plastic tape and a green plastic container. The navigator unfolds the note to check the address. The blocky felt pen writing has been smudged by his large sweaty thumb. Is that a six or an eight? Looks like a six. Definitely a six. He nods confidently.

Charlie Macintosh only has time to say "Hellooo...", before two thugs grab his arms and Wee-G winds a length of tape around his mouth. Then, in a single fluid motion, he is forced to sit on the parquet floor and zip-tied to the leg of the heavy oak sideboard.

Wee-G fusses with the entry intercom system and then they leave. Wee-G is the last one out. He turns and says to Charlie, "Payback traitor!" and slams the apartment door shut.

Charlie's panicked breathing rasps through his nose, but otherwise his apartment is silent. He sees two wires twisting their way from the carcass of the intercom and down the spout of a green 5-litre petrol container.

He scans around to see if anything in his reach can help: a Lladró figurine, a glass decanter, and a framed picture of his dad, arm draped around his uncle. Happier times. Felix makes an entrance. If there is anything less helpful than an empty decanter, it is this cat.

Outside a DPD delivery van comes to a stop. The driver checks his hand-held to confirm parcel and address. Apartment 6F, top left. He makes to press the buzzer and hesitates – the building's front door is left open. That's handy, he thinks to himself. He climbs three flights and knocks on the apartment door. No reply. He places the parcel against the door, photographs it and leaves. Back down the stairs and, as he exits the building, he makes sure to close the front door firmly. Safer that way, he reflects, in a self-satisfied way.

Two Jehovah's Witnesses in cheap black suits, pristine white shirts and black laminated badges hover. Which apartment to try first? Brother Wayne is less confident than Brother Barry and hangs back, thinking, this whole thing is an utter waste of time. Brother Barry mentally brushes down his spiel and presses the buzzer.

The two jump and glance at each other as the Harley Davidson backfires before it disappears around the corner.

"Jesus!" exclaims Brother Wayne.

A pause. "Yeah?" a disembodied voice mumbles.

"Hello, friend, have you seen the light of our almighty Lord?"

"Fuck off and die," replies the voice aggressively.

Wayne glances at the name on the door buzzer – apartment 8F Dean Lancaster.

Next door at apartment 6F, Charlie has become even more frantic. He targets thought waves to force Felix to grab a wire. Felix is resistant.

He glances at the photo on the sideboard and thinks to himself, "What would Uncle Bob do?

In another part of town, Uncle Bob, otherwise known as Rabbie 'Burns' Macintosh, hands a roll of banknotes to Wee-G and smiles coldly as he thinks of the inflammatory message dispatched to Dean the 'waster' and his other rivals.

Back at Boyd Drive, a moped putters around the corner and parks close to the kerb. The motor grinds to a halt, farts and emits a cloud of black smoke as its engine is switched off. The driver takes off her helmet, pulls the moped up onto its stand, breathes in the diesel fumes and fluffs up her mop of red hair. Mari Patel checks the address again to confirm it's the next building along from Dean's apartment. She barks a quick laugh at the coincidence.

"Just get rid of this stodgy old crap then go and see him. Surprise my man and get me some lovin'," Mari does a little circular hand-led dance to herself. She opens the back box, removes the pizza container with its 'Bill's Pizza' brand on the lid and approaches the front door. She reaches out to ring the bell when, just at the same moment, the door is pulled open forcefully from the other side.

"Sorry luv, didn't mean to scare you," says a crumpled old woman. She drags a wheeled shopping trolley behind her while wrestling with the weight of the door.

"Thanks," Mari catches the door and dodges past her. The front door swings gently back into place and nestles against the door frame. The lock clicks as the door closes. Up the stairs to apartment 6F.

A DPD delivery parcel sits against the door. She knocks on the panel loudly. No reply although, although... she just about detects, something? A squeak? It's muffled but it's coming from the other side of the door. There is a letter box, so she holds it open with her hand and bends down to stare through the hole.

She sees a young man sitting in the hallway with his hands behind him. His hair is a mess, and his mouth is covered in a shiny brown tape. He is communicating furiously with his eyes, which seem to be trying to escape from his head while a bubble of snot expands then contracts out of a nostril. Balancing the pizza box on an outstretched arm, she leans her free shoulder against the door, turns the handle and pushes hard. It doesn't move. She reaches into her pocket and removes a plastic credit card. Mari slips the card into the edge beside where the lock is located and the door pops open. A tortoiseshell cat leaps over a green petrol can, scampers between her legs and runs out of the apartment. Mari staggers into the hallway and struggles to regain her balance while juggling the unwieldy pizza box. She steadies herself and stares down at Charlie. Charlie stares up at her with desperate eyes.

And then the door buzzer rings.

****

Rabbie 'Burns' MacIntosh is furious. Furious with Wee-G for getting the wrong address, furious that the plan had gone tits-up and furious with the idiot for ringing the doorbell. Bob hadn't even had time to try and stop him as they stood at the door mentally scrolling through options about what to do. Wee-G hadn't said a thing. He'd just reached out his finger and did it. As if ringing that bloody doorbell was a perfectly natural thing to do.

Rabbie howls at Wee-G then cringes. He closes one eye and looks skywards towards Apartment 6F with the other as he waits to see the smoke and flames, but nothing happens. Eventually a voice comes over the speaker.

"Yeah?"

"Who are you? Where's Charlie?" Rabbie asks.

"Charlie? Ah yes Charlie. He's erm, at least I guess it's Charlie, he's ah, he's kind of tied up. I'm delivering a pizza."

"Open the door," Rabbie commands.

****

They gather in the lounge. Rabbie MacIntosh sits wide legged on a straight-backed chair with his head in his hands. He takes out his mobile and snarls an order to whoever has answered.

Charlie lies on a small two-seater red vinyl settee gently picking at the glue residue that lines both sides of his face. Every so often he glances cautiously in Wee-G's direction. Mari clutches the pizza box and stands near the door while Wee-G hovers behind her in the doorframe.

"Eh, I didn't know who you were pal. No hard feelings?" says Wee-G to Charlie with an embarrassed smile.

Charlie says nothing and continues to pick at his face. The four of them go silent. Each with their own thoughts. Mari decides to take the initiative.

"Yeah, I mean, I think I should go now. You want this? It's probably gone all cold by now." Mari holds the pizza box out.

Rabbie gets up, snatches the box from her, returns to sit down, opens the lid looks up to appraise Mari, "And precisely what are you going to say about all of this, you know, if anyone asks?"

Mari swallows a breath and blurts, "Me? I don't know nothing. What the fuck could I know? Looks like an accident, yeah? And we stopped it. I mean, I suppose the cat really did that. I saw its leg catch on the wire. Knocked it out of that can. Super cat innit?"

The three others look at her.

"Yer phone is ringing," Wee G says.

Mari puts her hand in her right-hand pocket of her jacket and fingers the phone.

"Might be your boss at your pizza place wondering where you are," adds Charlie.

Mari places her other hand on her other pocket where her pizza phone sits quietly.

"Naaah, it's probably nothing," Mari says dismissively.

"Answer it! You never know it might be important," Rabbie voice darkens as he says this. He stares at Mari intently.

Mari stares back mesmerized and finds herself removing the phone from her pocket. She stares at the number on the screen. She takes a deep breath and presses answer.

"Why're you not picking up, stupid bitch," Dean's loud, nasty and familiar voice echoes out of the phone, past her ear and into the room.

Mari freezes, stunned. He's never called her a stupid bitch before and that's put her head in a spin. She hesitates not sure what to do.

Rabbie drops the pizza box on the floor, gets out of his seat and walks over to Mari. One by one he gently peels her fingers off the phone and takes it from her. Then he smiles and speaks into the mouthpiece.

"Well, well. Dean Lancaster. Do you fancy trying to guess who this is?" he hisses.

At the other end a click and a single tone. Rabbie smiles again and turns to Mari.

"So, you're his friend. A good friend perhaps? Or maybe a bad friend? Your choice." Rabbie's voice drips with an icy coldness.

"I don't know the geezer. I deliver pizzas." she squeaks.

Rabbie leans over, opens the pizza box and peels off a wedge which he jams in his mouth. He chews sending splatters of cheese and pizza crust towards Mari as he speaks. "He took some things of mine, and it wasn't pizzas. Are you going to help me, or are you in my way? What else do you deliver or does my associate Wee-G have to search you? He's good at that."

She stares wide eyed at first Rabbie and then towards Wee-G. After a pause her shoulders slump. She takes the zippy bag out of her pocket and holds it towards Rabbie. Rabbie ignores it and nods his head at Wee-G.

Wee-G walks up to Mari and snatches the bag from her hand.

She fumbles a cigarette from a packet and lights it with her disposable lighter. The glowing cigarette shakes as her hand trembles.

The door buzzer rings again.

As Rabbie walks through into the hallway past the green petrol can towards the front door he says, "I can guess who this is."

He presses the intercom and shouts, "Come on up guys and bring your gear."

Then he strides slowly back into the lounge past a visibly apprehensive Mari, the smirking Wee-G and a worried looking Charlie.

Two minutes later there is a knock on the door.

"Come on in boys, the door is open." calls Rabbie. There is no answer.

"I don't think any of this is good Uncle Bob. Can't we just tidy everything away and get on with things?" Charlie whines softly.

"That's what I'm doing. Tidying everything away." Rabbie replies. "Why don't you make some tea?"

He calls again, "Clocks ticking, shift your fat arses and get in here boys. Time is money. Oh and watch out for that bloody can of petrol."

The door into the lounge opens slowly, and a head appears around the edge.

"Hello... Hello, have you seen the light of our almighty Lord?" asks Brother Barry tentatively.

Mari is quick but not quick enough. As she darts towards the door, Wee-G grabs a handful of her hair. She doesn't even pause and keeps going, seizes Brother Barry by the hand, and kicks over the petrol container. As they leave the front door, she flicks her cigarette over her shoulder back into the lobby of the apartment.

Inside Wee-G stares at the red wig in his hand and watches the back of the green haired girl disappear towards the staircase before a ball of flame takes over the hallway.

Mari and Brother Barry clatter down the stairs and out of the front door to meet three police cars – lights flashing. An officer is already on his radio calling for the fire brigade. The detective who arrests her is very familiar. Mari last saw him at her interview, when she started working and although he wears the same black tee-shirt, his tattoos and tongue piercing have vanished. This is the man who gave her a phone when she started her shift to keep in touch the delivery company. He grins expansively now as he retrieves it and waggles it at her with eyebrows raised, before sliding it into an evidence bag. A record of her travels.

In the back seat of a police car a handcuffed Dean fumes head down, caught as he ran in a panic out of his front door straight into the arms of the waiting officers. Outside number 8,

Brother Barry squats on a low wall, hyperventilating, while Brother Wayne fans him with a copy of the Watchtower. Beside them a tortoiseshell cat purrs loudly. An old lady holding a shopping trolley strokes the cat's ears and coos, "What a load of fuss, Felix. None of my business really and certainly nothing to do with a sweetie like you."

Philip is a retired university lecturer from Paignton in Devon, UK. He started writing short stories just before the pandemic and was runner-up in the Crowvus ghost story competition and the Jane Austen competition and long listed for the Alpine Fellowship Writing Prize and the Exeter Writers short story competition.

CRIMSON FOR CRIMSON

By Adam Shakinovsky

Aisha swallowed a blackberry and crimson juice burst in her mouth. It calmed her. The grainy innards coated her tongue. The overflow pooled purple beneath. This would be a quick stop before she collected her group. People easily got lost in the forest and today had to go well.

The organisers and their friends often had little real interest in foraging. They paid for one thing but, at a given point, made a play for another. Something she never wanted to give. Something that, when pressed, she always did. "Not today."

These words floated on foggy breath towards a curious doe. Eyes brim-full of starlight, it watched Aisha's words evaporate into the cold.

The times she had failed, Aisha had felt cheap. Helpless. She'd tried manners, genuflecting, earnest pleas. In return she had been ignored, laughed at, rolled over. Reason is nothing against a herd. "Not...today".

Quickly now. She slid back the sleeves of her shirt and wound the blackberry brambles around her forearms. Red thorns punctured her dark palms. Aisha's blood seeped, drip-like, into the short-combed spikes. She would give before she took. Crimson for crimson.

When the vines were sated, the same moment she felt she had given enough, they released each other. Firm friends who had visited together. To anyone else, the pattern of fruit on the bush was unremarkable. But to Aisha, it was a map pointing her to the secret heart of the plant. She reached inside, the thorns taking care not to harm her.

The tips of her fingers tickled coal-black berries. They seemed to pulse in her hands. Seven of them tumbled effortlessly into her oversized coat pocket. I won't need them. She promised herself.

"Are you Aisha?" the male voice strained across the expanse. A tribe of Sparrows fled for the clouds. The doe bolted, unseen.

Aisha ran across the copper leaves, puffing. Icy air filled her mouth, clearing her mind. The mist lifted a little as she reached the seven men. "Hello. You found us, ok?" she smiled.

"Eventually. This place is in the middle of nowhere!"

Groups like this always sent the polite one out first. He looked like a Moomin.

"I'm Malcolm. These are the boys."

Cheery, cheeky greeting grunts. Tall, angular-jawed boarding school types. She could imagine them saying "Very good, headmaster" with a respectful nod, and then wink at the new Biology teacher in the hope of a three-minute scuttling after class. "Nice threads. I love how you just don't care!" Was this negging? Did it ever work?

He was so lanky his shadow bullied sunlight from the grass it covered.

'Thanks. I just put on what I find."

"What if you find nothing?"

"Oh…I…I usually…"

"Joking…Joking!"

Aisha knew she looked like a high-fashion scarecrow with her mismatched colours and sizes. She watched an earthworm disappear into the mud. Lucky thing. Daring to look up again, she marvelled at the man's Hugo Boss overcoat.

"That's gorgeous." She said, meaning it.

"This? Bought it in Seattle. Pricey as hell, but, you know…"

"Oh." I don't.

"Do you always wear men's clothes?" This? Still?

The group's collective gaze pressed in. An unconscious circle had formed around Aisha. Everything she wore looked donated. Her 'outfit' exposed things she'd rather hide, or accentuated things she'd prefer remain anonymous. They hung from, or clung to, her elven caramel frame.

"Oh no – it's just…Like I say... I wear what I find..."

One of them noticed that her top button was missing. For Aisha it was an inconvenience that let the cold in. For him, it was an entry point. Somewhere he could start peeling...

She knew these looks. She feared these looks. Aisha folded her arms. Scars teach. Scars remind. But scars can rarely protect us. Quiet, she urged. Not today.

She hoisted a cheerier tone, "Let's head to the start of the trail, shall we?"

She moved off, they followed. Aisha stroked her hidden blackberries. One, two, three… She breathed deeply, caressing all seven before she began…

"Welcome to foraging, everyone. I'm Aisha, I'll be your guide. I've provided a basket for each of you and your treasures today. Perhaps as I hand them out, you could tell the group what brought you here."

Even to real foragers, Aisha knew this was a bland ice-breaker. Still…she was nervous and…well…if it flushed out the truth early, could she ask them to leave?

Smirks. Sheepish grins…"I've always wanted to try nettle tea."

Ok. That wasn't definitely sarcasm.

"I like nature." Chimed another. Hmmmm.

"I'm trying to eat less meat." Ah, Malcolm. Meek; furtive-eyed. As though he knew this would cause derision amongst the flock. And it did. Hoots. Jeers. Aisha would have accepted his sincerity had it not wafted over in a mist salted thick with bacon.

Aisha watered her hope. After all she was a professional. In fact, though her 23 years had passed living almost entirely hand to mouth, Aisha considered herself an optimist.

They trotted after her as she pointed out, with love, the surrounding magic and philosophy. Berries, herbs, patience, gratitude. As if to assist her, a breeze lifted crisp leaves to reveal a stunning set of Dahlias.

"This isn't a poorly stocked supermarket. It's an Odyssey. A conversation. Where, if you look, you could find everything you need for the rest of your life. Where you begin as one creature and end as another."

She sounded corny, meaning every syllable. The men parroted with inflected enthusiasm. They carried their little baskets. They placed in little herbs. Like farcical wolves bursting out of Little Red's tiny cloak. One of them kicked a fallen Woodpecker egg, nearly slipping on the ooze.

Whenever she looked back, she hoped to see them craning their necks at a Robin in a high branch. Or stooping to marvel at the purple Monkshood, Bellflowers and Fat Hen.

But each time she caught them just as they were looking away from her. Veering guiltily from the same eye-line. Their sights were fixed. On how she walked. On each supple, gliding curve. They can change. Give them time.

'Ow!' A bramble had latched onto the closest perv. He extricated himself with some difficulty and more than a little resentment. The forest was losing patience.

Before lunch, ham-handed, the gang frantically rubbed sticks together to claim Fire-Maker. Olympian masturbators duking it out for bronze. Aisha gently pressed herbs in her hand. Soaked in the scent of sage. She licked the first flakes of snow.

She stirred her pan of pesto. The meal marked the end of their experience so, if there was going to be an approach, it would be around now.

Maybe it won't come. Perhaps beneath their blank expressions and stifled yawns they were enchanted. The majesty was sinking in. Rain soaked up by soil. Invisible but nourishing.

She squeezed her eyes shut then opened them to the autumnal canopy above. Her prayers clambered upward on silver birches without branches. The falling flurry began to settle on her clothes.

"We've heard…"

Her heart sank. The smell of belly and rind still lingered on Malcolm.

"And tell me if I'm wrong…"

Wooden spoons scraped wooden bowls. Not, she thought, out of politeness. But to let her know that her hospitality was wanting. They haven't had enough.

"But…I understand you know where to find deer..."

Damn it. Malcolm gingerly held a peeping pile of cash.

"It isn't hunting season…" she began.

They were around her again. Nothing unconscious about it this time. Their breath, hot and hard, misted around her so it was all smoke, lips and teeth.

"You've done it for others-"

"We didn't come for the nettles-"

"We're willing to pay-"

An angry crow took off from a high branch, making it sway. Snow shook, sliding down several shirts. Their owners shivered. But they were undeterred.

"We won't tell anyone-"

"We've got money."

"There's no one around here for miles."

It was this last comment that scared her. She was alone. She had tried persuasion out of this before. She had been worn down. She had been overpowered.

She wished the snow would cloak her. She followed a flake from the eye of a man down to the mottled white and brown mud. Have I lost them? Did I ever have them?

They knew they had won. Now there was real fire sweeping through the group. Zips flew up on their oversize bags as the men sprang to life for the first time.

"Your phones stay with me until after." She offered up a bag in trembling hands. She bluffed insistence. They saw a beggar.

"But…"

"If anyone finds out…I'll lose my job."

Their annoyance mingled with pity. They could see she must have been given her clothes. That she was thin as a ragdoll. For her, foraging wasn't a cute hipster hobby. It was how she sustained herself in every way. And business must be slow.

Sulkily, they dropped their phones into the bag. Malcolm held out the sweaty wad of notes. Six months' rent, easy.

She walked past the money. Malcolm's confusion showed.

"Hang on..."

"I only take what-"

"But you're in a bad way, anyone can see that, and fair's fair."

Fair? Even the bribe wasn't fair. If she accepted it, what else would they want included in the budget? What else would they believe they'd bought? Her head throbbed, but all she said, indicating the forest, was: "This is yours as much as mine." She could see that it turned a few of them on.

The sky dripped a bucketful of blood-red light onto the whitening forest floor.

Rifles, dark-wooded, keen-sighted, unpacked and assembled almost by themselves.

Hail peppered the 'hunters' hands, taking aim at their eyes as well. They felt hardier. As though they were taking on the elements.

They sped through the undergrowth, pretences at politeness fallen away. Aisha tried to distract them. "Look, collared earthstar" she pointed, pointlessly. Hoping against hope that one of them would be dazzled by its brilliance and bring a halt to all this.

Silence. Titters. Gone were the half-hearted refrains of 'oh, I see!' No. They had used up their patience for foreplay. The Inkcaps and Earthballs watched on. Fungal witnesses to yet another of her failures. The snow covered them. Drawing a veil over what they were about to witness.

The men giggled. Giddy. Convinced they had cajoled (not threatened). Aisha stopped them. "We're close now."

Aisha held out the seven berries, black as the cosmos, to her captors. "For luck." Her sorrow cracked and leaked into the bowl of despair that became her stomach. Mechanically, they groped her offering from her hands. Thoughtless. Thankless.

"Sorry. The boys can get a bit carried away. All good fun, though." Malcolm proffered the cash again. She stared at it blankly.

"You smell surprisingly good." The man with the Hugo Boss coat leaned in, elbowing Malcolm out the way. "I like how natural you are. You know? I'm staying nearby tonight."

A few of his jackals grinned.

"Nowhere nearer than right here…"

Hugo Boss smiled at the semi-joke, gazing at Aisha. He raised his eyebrows and popped his blackberry in his mouth with a wink.

"Jesus Christ." He spat.

"That's disgusting!"

Their maws foamed with dark sticky gunk. They guzzled water but their lips and chins were irrevocably coated.

Aisha walked ahead. She looked back, motioning them

forward to a clearing. There, looking somehow out of place, were seven stags.

Spitting and still annoyed, the men moved into position. Twigs snapped, leaves rustled, branches creaked. Actual hunters would have questioned why the stags stood oblivious. Half-heartedly chewing grass. Listlessly licking snow.

Rifles raised. Steadied. Aimed. "Bored bastards."

The shots were unremarkable. Unambitiously close to their targets. The 'hunters' quarry, such as they were, flopped onto, and into, the snow. It piled onto them in flurries.

They ran over to claim their kill, whooping and hollering as they went.

Aisha narrowed her eyes. It was time to get low.

The men pawed and kicked at the layers of white and red-stained powder. They expected to see sodden, matted fur. Broken antlers. Bloodied hooves. Black eyes staring vacantly into the void. But only the latter met them.

Confusion. Dry mouths. Adrenaline. Each of them was looking at the thing they had shot. Yet none of them could have shot these men who lay coiled or spread stupidly at their feet. Where were the deer?

These were flesh sacks who, moments ago, had been deer more adequately than they had ever been humans. The 'hunters' turned, skittish, guns raised towards Aisha. They screamed at her, panicked when they couldn't see her. She watched through watering eyes as shots fired her way. Bark splintered off oak nearby, the trees taking damage in her place.

The guns held in hands that shook. The men's thoughts ran into each other as they charged as one back towards Aisha.

...tricked...that bitch...we're going ...she's going to jail...there's more of us...it's our word against...why's the gun slipping...? Why's my face furring...what's breaking through my boots...?'

The metamorphosis looked excruciating. Bone tore through eyeballs. Cartilage ripped through soft belly. Antlers shredded cheeks and lips. Flesh split like grape-skins. The men turned into the creatures they thought they had killed in bone-breaking, bone-aching slow motion. They were split, bent, stretched and then swallowed by their new forms, soaked entirely in purple-crimson slush and sinew.

Ravens screeched to cover the shrill uncontrollable begging and baying of the Damned and Deforming.

The last gun slipped from the last hoof. The final antlers fully formed and fanned out. Their wracking and retching complete, the new wrought 'deer' saw their surroundings through bloodshot eyes.

Aisha walked among them. She picked up the cash. Claimed every item of real quality that she found. This included one barely split, slightly scratched Hugo Boss jacket. She would mend it. It would last and be loved.

The human corpses were changing in the snow. Flaking away, chalky, in the wind. As she watched them merge with the ether, Aisha remembered she would need to get rid of the phones in her bag.

The thought of tomorrow's task, a new group, weighed heavily on her. She stroked her new friends. Her replacement deer. Comforted them.

"I'll try again. You'll be safe tomorrow."

She nuzzled up close to one. Her nose to his snout.

"I'll convince them, you'll see. The forest will be enough for them. You mustn't worry."

She never knew exactly how much he had understood of what she said. But looking into his onyx eyes, she recognised blind fear when she saw it.

Adam Shakinovsky lives in England and is the co-author of OneTrackMinds, an anthology of stories about life changing songs. He is also a speaker, and producer of television and theatre. He loves to write about friendship, create new myths, and explore what happens when kindness is mistaken for weakness.

A GIFT FROM THE SEA

By Caroline Quigley

He was a gift from the sea, emerging from the jaws of defiance. I could only stare at Mother Nature's most precious pearl, half-dead yet half alive, as he stumbled and fell; the saltwater patiently choking him.

I stood still, not knowing what to do. His uniform gave him away. He was German and this was 1944 on Achill in the West of Ireland. It was nearing the end of the war and even though Ireland had remained neutral there was no love lost for Germany's side. My own family were from Dublin and listened daily to the radio, more times than not cheering when the American and English allies won a battle or gained precious lost ground. In our hearts we knew the war would be over soon, as Germany's defeat was inevitable, we hoped that victory and peace would come as soon as possible. And yet there he was like a beautiful siren, floating helplessly in the water. A merman that somehow was sent to entice me.

I could see him gasping for breath as he swallowed yet another mouthful of water, as wave after wave towered over him. And then I heard it; soft, distant and subtle at first, a deep haunting melody. My heart almost stopped with fright, but then my soul suddenly filled with the most beautiful, peaceful sadness that turned into joy. It was the call of the *seala* or seal. It was known that some people on the islands of Skye and Iona, off the coast of Scotland, called them *selkies*, half-human, half seal, because of their song. It was mesmerising to hear it, you almost felt blessed as it seemed somehow sacred. It was a primal longing that resonated deep within my soul; one of love, grief and despair.

It was the call of the *seala* that had prompted me forward. At first, my legs were heavy in the sand, yet they seemed to have a mind of their own as they started to move. Then I was running. The coldness of the seawater stung my skin and, like a sharp slap, it awakened a warrior spirit in me as I kept moving carefully onwards.

I could see my siren, limp and barely breathing, trying desperately to keep his head above water. I swam cautiously over to him; he was barely breathing. I gently held his head above the water, and he gratefully opened and closed his eyes as if to say 'thank you'. It was only fleeting, but that first look would stay in my soul forever. His glassy, green eyes glistened brightly against his strong cheekbones, set gently against the contours of an elegant nose. Too elegant for a man, I thought, as it made him look almost angelic.

I tried to move him onto his back to help him float but he was tall and heavy set. Soon, he would be under the water. I felt that I was only momentarily alleviating his suffering, prolonging the inevitable. I cried out for help to anyone who could hear me, fishermen, villagers, even *selkies*; too terrified to move or my siren would be gone, devoured by the sea's hungry jaws. After what seemed like an agonising wait, I saw a piece of driftwood bobbing up and down, almost like a crocodile looking for new prey. I realised it had come off his boat, which had smashed against the rocks. My breath quickened as I shouted "HOLD ON," then somehow, by loosening my right hand, I managed to grasp the driftwood as his head sank under the water again. I knew I needed to retrieve the wood, as it was my only chance, so I let him go and grasped it. He bobbed up and down for a minute and started to sink. By now I had a firm hold on the wood, so, by grabbing his legs, I managed to place the piece of driftwood directly under him, eventually pulling up his head. He was barely moving. Luckily the tide was with us and we reached the shore. As I dragged him off the wood, I noticed the muddy sand hung from our bodies and faces almost as if we had just been born from out of our earth mother.

"BREATHE" I shouted, gently slapping him and placing him on his side. I slowly pressed my hands on his lungs. "BREATHE," I screamed. I then placed my cold lips against his salty, sandy blue ones. Even though we were both cold, and almost half alive, the flame that ignited between us was unmistakable. I was now giving him the kiss of life, pouring my cold, hot breath into his mouth and lungs. I pinched his nose and opened his mouth, mine upon his, desperately trying to revive him.

"BREATHE," I shouted out again, then just "breathe please", I pleaded with him before I started to cry. I was exhausted, spent, I felt cheated, all this for nothing, my beautiful siren. "NO,", I defiantly said, he wasn't giving up that easily, and something then took over me, a wild instinct, another force, like a primate I pounded his chest: "BREATHE SIREN MAN,

BREATHE." I collapsed face down on the sand, only for a muffled sound to emerge, followed by a short cough. My siren was moving at last, spluttering and spitting out the sand and saltwater. Eventually, he reached his hand out to me. "Danke schön," he muttered.

I still don't know how I did it, as later it all seemed like a distant haze, but somehow I managed to drag him on the driftwood back to my little cottage that was conveniently hidden down a little lane near the beach. Earlier on I had felt quite warm and needed a walk in the sea air when I saw him, luckily it was getting dark and I was the only person on the beach at the time.

The cottage was small with just two rooms, a kitchen cum sitting room, a small hall and bedroom that veered off the sitting room and a shed-like toilet and washroom outside. This little cottage had been in my family for generations and had become my little getaway holiday house for years. It had been passed down from my great-aunt Sissy and when my uncle's big house on the island became too much, I would retreat here, to think, paint and write, dreaming of worlds between worlds, my own life, wants and desires. The cottage always held a special place in my heart. Every time I had to make a decision I came here. It was almost like a rite of passage.

My siren muttered something as I poured fresh water into a cup for him to drink. "Easy, easy," I said, as he gulped down the freshwater. I carefully washed his face. It is as if he was chiselled by Leonardo himself, I thought, and I smiled at this. He couldn't be more than thirty, yet deep down I knew that I needed to hide him. His jacket had all the German markings of rank on it and I knew he was a pilot. I then decided to make a small bonfire on the beach to burn the jacket. Only his shirt and trousers remained. I knew my brother had left some clothes in the old chest of drawers when he had previously stayed and I was glad of them now. I laid them on the bed and closed the door. Best to let him sleep, I thought. Strangely I had no fear it was as if I'd known him all my life.

As I stretched out on the small armchair in front of the fire, observing the glowing embers I wondered what had happened to him. Who was he? And why had be been put in my path? All of these and other questions would be answered in the morning. Right now I knew I desperately needed sleep after my excursion, so I started to drift away gently, comforted by the firelight.

It was barely 6 o'clock in the morning and the sun was just starting to set. I walked over to the little window and saw a silhouette appear on the horizon. It was human; my beautiful siren was bathing naked at the beginning of the seashore. As I looked out at him, he seemed only part human and part ethereal. His creamy skin shone against his golden hair and his long, muscular legs moved slowly in the water. Even though his back was to me, I knew in my soul he was silently calling out to me; I could just feel it. His presence tugged at my heartstrings. I threw my cardigan on and I walked along the shore, my long nightgown trailing behind me. The water was warm and small crabs nipped at my ankles. He stopped and turned around when he saw me. We both just stared at each other. Then my siren beckoned me forward. Diligently I obeyed. I was mesmerised yet excited by this otherworldly experience. We did not need to speak for we knew the truth of it. Sometimes there are no words for what passes between two human beings in love.

In practical terms, I had known him for only moments, but in our presence together we had known each other for centuries, even lifetimes before. I waded waist-deep into the lukewarm water, shivering slightly as he watched every part of me. His eyes were like glowing emeralds in the morning dawn. All was still as he touched my face, electricity passing between us. I held his hands, our fingertips burned together and we saw each other's souls; our lips then locked and I knew we were home.

He kissed every part of me, delighting in my many freckles and moles; they were the softest yet most intense kisses I had ever known. His breath made hot circles on my body. I placed my hands on his chest, softly at first then like a greedy child wanting more candy. And still, we didn't speak. As morning dawn finally arrived it was as if Mother Nature had bestowed her blessings upon us. We were now inseparable, two sirens in their Mother's salty womb.

Soft waves washed over us as we lay there for what seemed like hours. We knew that we would remember this moment for the rest of our lives. I wanted to always keep it close, remembering every precious detail, as I let the memory of our love soak into every pore of my being. I could now feel his heart beating next to mine, a beautiful sonata of sound. It was calling me. Such perfection is rare, I thought.

We knew in time it would all change. He was a deserter, he didn't believe in war, and had two small children back in Germany. But for that moment, we were here wrapped around each other. I decided to just be present and accept my fate.

"Robert," he muttered.

"Maggie." I smiled.

Then I heard it again, the call of the *seala*, the song of the *selkie*, echoing, searching, and reaching. I knew they were singing a fateful lullaby for us, as if they knew, they just knew.

Caroline is an Irish author inspired by people, history, landscapes and the natural world. She started to write in 2010, with a previous background was in the arts, theatre and film, and I also worked in holistic medicine. Her first book 'An Angel Calling' (non-fiction) continues to sell through Amazon.

A STRANGER'S LOOKOUT

by Charlotte West

Last summer, Elle and I got into a routine of driving down to the beach each day after work. Even when it rained, as it often does on England's southwest coast, we still would sit in the carpark, overlooking the sea and talking about nothing in particular.

Mostly, we were lucky that year; the sun beat down on our skin with heavy urgency. We would stay until sunset, every night marvelling at the vibrancy of the sky, as if we hadn't seen its familiar display the night before. We were constantly awed by Mother Nature's eclectic shades of watercolour as they washed over the sky - how could she do so much with so little? We fell into a deep, philosophical place on those nights, as if we were in conversation with Mother Nature herself.

Near the end of the season, on a Thursday in late August, we had settled down into our spot on the pebbles. Elle was lying face down, drenched in tanning oil as she longed to get her skin the colour of Love Island contestants. Meanwhile, I was sitting upright with a book in my hands, factor 50 sunscreen smeared across the few slithers of skin that I dared to show and often adjusting my knee-length shorts.

We were 24: Elle stuck in a retail store till 5pm, me working in a corporate office that pumped air conditioning into our lungs like it was an oxygen mask - the sole thing keeping us upright at our desks. We fled eagerly to the sea every night to feel the sensation of real air flushing round our lungs and the blanket of heat on our skin.

Even though this was a new daily routine for us, we'd been coming to that corner of the beach since we were teenagers. That spot had captured our attention once we realised that no matter the tide, its distance from the sea was ideal. We would never get swept away if the tide was in, and we had a nice amount of strut distance when the tide was out. It was also a healthy separation from the flurry of tourists gathered near the end of the beach too - just so much that they were out of earshot, but we could still feel part of the evening hustle and bustle, where BBQs and paddle boards were aplenty.

We had been coming here so often, that there was an unspoken rule between locals that this side of the beach required a four-metre radius between everyone's spot. It was just good manners. That was until that Thursday night, when a young couple came to sit just a couple of steps away from us. I sighed into my novel, as I could see in my peripheral vision, they were laying down their towels - the sanctity of the evening ruined.

A few minutes later, I found myself watching them from behind my sunglasses as they peeled their layers away. Their pasty city-dwelling skin finally being met with coastal sun.

The woman looked up, catching my eye with a smile, "we're going for a quick swim, can you watch our stuff?"

I smiled back and nodded, hoping I was radiating the same warm energy that we naturally radiate in the summer. She looked grateful as she jumped up, her blonde hair tied haphazardly into a ponytail, and her coral bikini looking vibrant in the evening light. She grabbed her partner's hand and pulled him to his feet. They began skidding their way across the pebbles, hopping from foot to foot in a joyous ache as the pebbles dug into their skin. They entered the water and squealed with delight at the refreshing shock of its unfamiliar cold bite. Around them were others, locals, who did a slow gentle shuffle as they waded through the water. Their fingertips traced along the surface, smoothing the coolness along their forearms and breathing deeply to get control over the chill. They glanced up at the couple, whose squeals were echoing around the bay, but they were oblivious to being so out of place.

I lay my book down on the towel in front of me and turned to Elle. "It's funny, isn't it? How they trust a stranger to stop anyone stealing their things."

Elle was silent, but she turned to face me signalling she was rousing herself from a sunbathing trance. I kept talking. "Like, who are they protecting their things from? Surely the likelihood of someone stealing from them when there are so many witnesses is pretty slim."

Elle leant up on her elbow, sliding her sunglasses down from her forehead so she could see me properly. "What's all this talk about 'logically'? You've never made a logical decision in your life."

"Well, that's kind of my point," I breathed. "I wouldn't ask anyone to watch my stuff. I'd either hide it, or not bring anything I would miss in the first place."

"You're the epitome of innocence, Lissa - you're reading a book by Jane Austen, of course they've chosen you to keep guard."

"Some of the most dangerous people in the world look innocent on the outside. Did you not watch Inventing Anna?"

"Most people have more faith in humanity than you do."

"You're missing the point."

"I don't think you had a point in the first place," she said, placing her head down on her arms again.

I looked ahead at the shoreline, scanning for the couple that had put their trust in me. I spotted them with their arms wrapped around one another's neck, occasionally splashing each other and screaming in glee. Watching them, I thought, maybe it was trust that encouraged people to do the right thing - that handing over of responsibility in the hope that people would come through.

I picked up my book again, nestling my attention back into Austen's world, when I felt Elle shift beside me. She sat up, looked out towards the sea, and then back to me - a wicked grin plastered across her face.

My skin got goose-bumps. I knew that grin. That grin

interfered with our friendship regularly. It was that grin that often made me consider moving out of the flat we shared and facing the world alone. It is for that reason, I think, that Elle liked using that grin on me so often. She knew it pulled me out of my soil, when all I wanted was for my roots to sink lower into the ground.

She threw a shirt over her tanned shoulders and skipped over to the couple's belongings, rifling through the open tote bag. Her eyes were daggers, sharply scanning each item she came across, weighing up their relevance to our neighbour's lives. Her manicured nails began lightly slipping between the objects.

"Elle!" I hissed at her. My eyes were darting between her slender back and the couple splashing around in the water.

I saw her fist clasp something palm-sized and in a moment, she was sauntering back to me, as if nothing had happened.

"What the hell was that?" I accused, my breath sitting heavy in my chest.

She opened her fingers like a clam shell, and there lay a lipstick, its golden case glinting in the sunlight and screaming expense.

I was breathless, "oh my God, you can't take that! Put it back right now! Please Elle!"

"Chill out, Lissa. They're city folk, they can afford a new lipstick. She won't notice until she gets home and then she'll just assume it fell out anyway. It's really not a big deal."

"If it's not a big deal then what's the point in taking it?"

Elle considered this for a second, turning the lipstick over in her palm with a look of adoration. "It gives life a bit of a thrill, don't you think?"

I rolled my eyes and returned to my book once again, only to find that my brain couldn't process the words; they were getting interrupted by panicked thoughts. Beside me, Elle returned to rest peacefully on the pebbles, as if nothing had happened. Unease bubbled up through all my muscles, my knee bouncing on the ground, anticipation and guilt churning together in my stomach like butter.

Finally, I heard giggles drifting up the beach and knew the couple were on their way back to us. I looked over at Elle who had hid the lipstick under her towel, folding it into a pillow and resting her head on top. My eyes continued to bore into the ivory pages of the Penguin classic in my hands.

Dripping bodies appeared beside us, and the couple collapsed onto their towels in a heap of smiles. The guy leaned over his girlfriend to catch our attention, "Hey, thanks girls!" he said, his mousy brown hair soaking wet from having dunked his head in the sea. I gave him a weak smile. This was not unusual behaviour for me, remaining mute was always my default behaviour around strangers. Still, this silence felt like social suicide - they were onto us, I was sure.

I glanced at Elle, who gave me a wink. She got a thrill from putting me in uncomfortable situations. You might call that a bad friend, but I would call her a sister. She knew how to make me live - even tiny thrills of adrenaline, such as this, was enough to pry me out of my shell. Without her, I'd always leave the party early, or never go at all, and that's no way to be young.

Soon I heard some disgruntled mumbling from beside us and the rummage of belongings in a tote bag. Silently, breathlessly, I put down my book and got to my feet. Striding to the water's edge. My eyeline fixated on the horizon ahead and I stumbled on the pebbles a few times from my unshakeable sense of panic.

Once I reached the water's edge, I let the ocean lap at my toes. I have always been one to turn a blind eye to uncomfortable situations. Ignorance is not just bliss, but paradise. Often there's just no need to feel the brace of courage in your chest.

Breathing deep, the water swept through the gaps in my toes with a tickle and my heels sank down into the wet sand. When the tide was low and the weather calm, the rhythmic nature of the sea helped calm my nerves.

A few minutes later, Elle's hand was on my shoulder, her face beaming with a smug smile. The tension in my body immediately seeped away and melted into the sand.

"Good karma is coming my way; I can feel it." I glanced at her unbelieving. "Oh, I gave it back to her, obviously. Told them I saw it in the sand, so it must've fallen out when they arrived. She didn't question anything, just relieved to have it back. It was a gift apparently. Designer. Christian Louboutin, I think she said. Anyway, they're having a BBQ later at their caravan and invited us along - want to come?"

"You're a bad person."

Elle shrugged, "I just make life happen, and the universe rewards me for that." She flashed me another bold grin and slipped her fingers in mine.

It's true - Elle had the ability to start a conversation anywhere and loved an experience that could then become a silly story to tell later.

She pulled me back up the beach and towards our camp, letting me leave my worries at the shoreline.

Except, when we reached the corner of the beach, our bags were gone.

And so were the couple beside us.

Charlotte is a 23-year-old writer based in Dorset, currently working in influencer marketing. She often takes inspiration from her beautiful coastline and explores the themes of home and human connection in her work. She can be found on Twitter @charlottewest99

A SPOON IN THE SOCKET

By Kit Derrick

The small boy slowly closes his eyes as he lays his head back on the warm pillow, the silence of the room punctuated by his slightly gasped breathing. His mind creates a new vision and the image he sees comes gradually into focus. His is facing a barrier of large, soft-edged, differently coloured blocks, seeming to appear out of the blackness and swirl in front of his presence, forming themselves into a bright, surreal, patchwork wall. One minute he is tiny at the foot of this softly pulsating wall, and then the next he is a huge giant, with the Lego-style bricks at his toes.

Sweating, the boy opens his eyes and coughs feebly, his gaze sweeping slowly over the panorama of the tinselled bedroom with its lovingly licked-together sugar-paper chains across the ceiling, blurry and out of focus. He can't quite remember why the decorations are up there, but it must be a celebration of some kind. The boy's right hand reaches down under the duvet to scratch his itchy testicles and under sleepy eyelids, he imagines watching the passage of his own hand, seeing the dark underside of his duvet, the soft blue and white pyjamas, and then the shadowy pinkness of his sweaty skin.

The boy's eyes blink and sink closed again. The immense psychedelic wall tilts and spins around him, like a fairground ride but without the nausea. His fringe sways in the breeze from the open window. The boy feels the wind become his mother's fingers, gently smoothing his wispy black hair back from his forehead. He lays still, half-smiling at the sensation, hoping it won't stop.

He drifts in and out of sleep, the hallucinations and dreams mixing until reality and imagination blur into one and he no longer notices the difference, just accepts what will be will be, and lies sweating, sniffing, and listening to his own shallow breaths. But he doesn't like the sound of the breathing. It doesn't sound happy to his ears, and he wants to hear only happy sounds.

He forces himself to concentrate on what he can perceive beyond his own body; listens, tries to hear the noise of the grass growing in the back garden outside his window. He thinks it sounds like tissue paper being rustled and that is a good sound. He pictures the thin stems pushing upwards through the clay soil, stretching tensely towards the light, making the lovely rustling noise. Fascinated, his mind watches the green stalks thicken and intertwine, then gently fade back into a huge barrier, and the boy is back in his bed, staring up towards the infinity of coloured bricks from the foot of the wall. He thinks he can see small invisible things climbing up and down the brickwork. He's forgotten the grass, and the small, invisible things are happy he thinks, so he isn't scared of them. The patterns of the glowing bricks are addictive, and he tries to follow the order, as he does on his Simon toy, where you press buttons to remember a sequence of lights. He hasn't played with that toy since the previous Christmas.

There is a change, to atmosphere and to surroundings as the boy hears raised voices, familiar voices he thinks, and strains his ears to try and make out meaning from the sounds. But they're just sounds. And they don't matter except for the fact they distracted him from the game he was playing, of guessing a pattern. The bed floats sluggishly up the wall and the boy passes green bricks, red squares, bright orange rectangles. The bricks are rubber, jelly or concrete. He isn't too sure which, and it doesn't really matter, but they all look pretty, and belong just where they are. They pulse, like they agree with him, and the boy smiles in satisfaction that he's clever.

A jarring, unwelcome wailing starts to encroach on the peace. A human noise. The bed sinks regretfully to the foot of the wall, unwilling to float while the sound continues. The boy opens his eyes and rubs them absently. He looks wearily around the busy room, empty save for himself and the billowing curtains. And the noises. Under drooping eyelids, the boy can see a droplet of sweat following the contour of his nose, slowly rolling towards the tip. Everything else is forgotten for a moment except for the bead of liquid, as he waits for it to fall from the end.

His mother's head appears around the door, too low to be physically connected to her neck, which is most peculiar, though strangely not unexpected. The boy tries to focus his eyes on her, but the image remains fuzzy and impossible. The only clear feature he can see is his nose, and the bead of sweat. Noises come from his mother. Re-assuring noises, but just noises. The boy closes his eyes once more, comforted, and floats higher up the multi-coloured wall, out of his bed and upright now, clearly visible against the bright bricks, in his light blue and white striped pyjamas. He's flying, and extends his arms to the side for balance, and to steer.

The boy realises that the wall is inches from his face now, and notices that it is getting darker, more brown bricks now, darker shades. They're almost rubbing against his nose and this close, he can see that they're made of corduroy, which is funny for some reason. He is about to laugh when suddenly his dream-hand reaches upwards and finds the top of the wall. The boy coughs almost silently, expelling hot breath from between his baking and imperceptibly cracked lips. He grips the top of the wall and pulls himself upwards. His head reaches the top brick and with a supreme effort the boy forces himself higher, above that a layer of dark grey rubbery bricks, which aren't anywhere near as amusing as the fabric ones.

And everything is sideways.

There, right in the boy's field of vision, is the hall outside of his bedroom door; the dark blue carpet leading to the tidy kitchen with its chequerboard tiles at the far end, the bathroom door on the right, the door to the lounge on the left, and everything is crystal clear and sharply focused now, with no blurring or fuzziness. The only oddity is that that he is facing sideways, horizontal. It is quite strange, though doesn't seen unnatural or worrying. As he stares at the pile carpet, he becomes aware that perhaps his angle isn't the only unusual aspect. In fact, he realises, he is also currently about two inches above the carpet, stiffly perpendicular to the wall.

The sights in front of him seem normal, but there are also the noise-voices. There's something wrong with the noise-voices. They're currently buzzing, agitated, unhappy. He tries to ignore the unhappy sounds and returns his thoughts to what he can see. It is so nice not to be sweating any more, not to feel clammy, or over-warm. He searches for more details of the current situation, now that he is no longer in his bed, and sideways.

He's aware that he is tiny, perhaps ten inches long. Above his rigid, horizontal form, he has fantastically peripheral vision, and can discern the shape of a bed, and the top of a young boy's sweating head at the farthest end of the duvet, his face resting on a damp pillow. There is a shallow rasping of breathing, and two hands gripping the top of the fabric, which reminds him of a popular cartoon figure, a face and fingers looking over a wall, with the moniker 'Kilroy Was 'Ere.' That's funny. Behind him, he can feel a cool breeze against his... he can't work out what part of him that is.

Sluggishly, the boy in the bed forces open his eyes. He can distantly make out the sound of softer, more conversational, voices. He looks down over his quilted patchwork duvet and can almost focus clearly enough to see the large wooden serving spoon, jammed at right angles into the electric plug socket by his bedroom door. This is simultaneously surprising and yet makes perfect sense, explaining the earlier viewpoint. The boy sighs and lets his tired eyes droop closed, rolling snugly onto his side and pulling the warmth of the down-filled covering tight against his clammy skin. It feels cosy and re-assuring. The moment his eyelids slide down fully to close out the light, he is sideways once more, as he expected. He can see a pair of blue rolled down socks and ankles in sandals this time. There is another set of ankles facing them, just beyond, in pink slippers with a fur trim.

The sounds floating down from above twist into meanings, and he realises that his mother's ankles are telling his father's ankles to go into the kitchen and make some tea. He wonders for a moment how ankles can complete this task, as the mugs live on a shelf far too high for them to reach, but mother's voice has no doubt thought of that. She always knows what to do. As it is father's ankles, and not mother's, making the drinks, then mother must have something more pressing to do. He knows it must be important if it takes precedence over the making of tea. Tea is almost ritualistic in the house. His sister likes coffee, but it is too bitter for his own taste-buds, even with sugar and lots of milk.

Beyond the feet, the bathroom door is slightly ajar and he can sense rather than hear a gentle sobbing from within. The first pair of ankles, the ones with the socks, obey the instruction and walk diametrically away and into the kitchen, past his mother's slippered feet, which turn towards to the right. Something, he assumes her hands, pushes the hollow wood-effect door fully open, and the feet enter the bathroom. The door magically swings back behind them, but doesn't close, as it knows it must allow the boy to hear what is being said. It must be something important, and though he finds it hard to concentrate, or care, the boy tries to follow the sounds, and make sense of them.

As his father's socked and sandaled feet move further away in the kitchen, he can hear the noise of the kettle beginning filled and put on the hob to boil, the gas being lit. There are bare legs, hairy legs above the ankles, and long, blue, canvas shorts. He doesn't need to look any higher. He knows what his father looks like already, and he isn't the focus of what is happening. Emanating from the bathroom are soft, comforting noises, which he recognises as being his mother's voice. The sobs, his sister's sobs, are receding.

Random words and snatches of phrases float out of the bathroom and the sandals in the kitchen stop moving, straining to listen too.

The words make no sense, and he only recognises fragments. "The first time." "Proud." "Scary, I know, love." "It's okay." "Understand." "Just stay there a while." "Daddy won't come in." "Growing up." If he had eyebrows to lower into a frown, he would. They don't seem to make sense. But the voice is soft and soothing, and that sounds nice, and that's much more important than whatever they might mean. He hears a tight little laugh, a response to something he didn't catch, and it develops into low, quiet tears again.

The sandals in the kitchen pace around, like they don't know what to do or where to go, but the whistle of the kettle nearing boiling point suggests they just need to be patient and wait. That should be obvious. The vertical wooden serving spoon, securely balanced in the electrical socket in the wall, watches and tries to listen carefully but doesn't really understand.

Three clear words floats soothingly out from the noises, "It's perfectly normal..." and those words re-assure and make him realise that understanding isn't necessary. If his mother's voice says that this is perfectly normal, then everything must be perfectly normal. After all, he's just a perfectly normal wooden spoon, watching events in the next room as his human body wriggles lower into his mattress, feeling a chill at the same time he reaches up and wipes the sweat from his forehead with his cotton pyjama sleeve.

The breeze blows strongly through the open window against the thick muslin curtains, and against the back of his concave wood. If it could smile, it would, now able to explain which part of it the wind is caressing.

He's been distracted, and missed the conclusion of the conversation, but watches his mother's slippers stride purposefully into the hall, somehow closing the bathroom door behind them, leaving it just slightly ajar, to hear any call of their titles as Mum and Dad. His mother's ankles join the set of sandaled feet in the kitchen, and the soft sobbing noises from the toilet in the bathroom start again, but gently, not afraid this time. Horizontal, he watches the slippered feet slowly walk towards, and then step carefully over him.

The mother stands at the foot of the bed and watches her boy wrapped up tight and snug in his duvet, his eyes scrunched tightly shut, sweat on his forehead, coughing weakly. It never rains but it pours. But maybe this is for the best. In his current state, he won't be aware and won't have questions, and it delays talking about things he doesn't need to know yet.

She pauses and just watches his face, wondering what he's dreaming about. She wants to tuck him in, although he doesn't need any more warmth. A half-smile teases up the corner of his lips, and she's reminded of him sleeping as a baby. It seems like only yesterday to her. With a glance over her shoulder, knowing she has a more pressing task, she eases her way around the bed, and slips her fingers through his wet and sticky hair, unplastering the strands from his forehead. She smiles.

The boy is slowly drifting lower down the multi-coloured wall of round, blue, bricks, which fascinate him. All thoughts of what he's seen have slipped away, never to return. Now, he is tiny at the foot of the huge wall, but upside down, defying gravity, inches from the dark pile carpet which has appeared. His lips curl in a smile. It's funny, being upside down. The world is turning upside down.

The breeze runs through his fringe, cooling his fevered brow.

Kit Derrick is an author and poet based in North-West England, with four novels currently available through all good bookshops and libraries. You can visit him and find out more online at www.kitderrick.com, or follow his thoughts on twitter @kitderrick1.

WIDOWED

By Ian Carass

There are fingerprint marks on the sideboard and Julia does not care. There are some casually scattered coins, a book of stamps, a lipstick, an empty coffee cup, and more, all abandoned on the sideboard. None of these has made it back to its assigned spot or keeping-place: to a drawer; to the old, ivy-patterned biscuit tin; to the third kitchen cabinet from the right; to the make-up bag in the bedside table; or wherever. It does not disturb Julia. He will never see this now.

In the mirror on the wall above the sideboard Julia adjusts her hair, teasing the curl, not a natural curl, into place. It hangs there to partially obscure the scar near her right eye. The scar has not faded in twenty years, it is still that pale, puckered line that runs very close to her eye. It could not be mistaken for a crow's foot, some wrinkle delved by laughter or sadness, that everyone has (or should have) past the age of fifty. But make-up and that curl, artfully arranged, lessen the impact.

Things could have been worse, Julia knows, but she is a quick learner. There was no repeat of that incident, the one that scarred her; there did not need to be. It happened early-on, maybe the week after they came home from the honeymoon; it was like lightning striking inside the house. Except that it was not random: it was not a bursting of atmospheric pressure; a release of pent emotions of anger, frustration or hurt. This was calculated, precisely timed, deftly achieved; it would be kept between them. The cut would not need stitching. The scar (really quite easily explained and brushed into obscurity) was the marker of the new compact.

Julia puts down her hairbrush and takes off her scarf. The room has darkened and it looks like rain outside and she would rather not go out now. There is nothing she needs really, there is no imperative driving her to the butcher or the chemist. Her cupboards and the fridge are adequately stocked (most of it is delivered to her door now) but the patterns of twenty years run very deep, rutted in her life. She will have an early night tonight.

The next day, mid-morning, the television is on, still a novelty in the daytime, but nothing much flickering across the screen keeps Julia's attention. Her late husband's gin delivery has arrived that day, early doors. He has had the stuff delivered for many years now, from a specialist distillery. Julia does not have a clue as to how to cancel the order; the paperwork that comes with the bottles is scant in detail. It is the same with the newspaper which comes every day. Julia does think to herself, frequently, How difficult could it be, to cancel the papers, cancel the gin. People do these things all the time, it surely cannot require any extraordinary gifts. Perhaps she has lost the knack of managing the day to day tasks of life, Julia wonders, the ordinary stuff. So still they come, and daily she finds herself turning the pages of the newspaper that drops through the letterbox, baffled by the bullying stupidity of people, the venality, the dishonesty. Julia would rather it did not come into her home, all this news from the world, but she turns the pages each morning, drinking her coffee, eating her toast (wholemeal, these days), getting buttery finger marks on every page.

Right up to the end, he had a gin or two every night, her late husband. Julia never partook.

When the very first bottle came out of his briefcase and he added a finger depth of it into a glass, he had turned to Julia.

"You won't have one, will you," he had said then, years ago, and he had said this, or something similar, many times down the years.

What could she have said to his remark? His words did not require a response, other than a smile of acquiescence. Julia reflects that most things were settled that way in their marriage and life together, big things and small things, without discussion, without hardly asking the question, or admitting that it was a question, some point of debate, a matter of choice or opinion: foreign holidays; fitted kitchens; skimmed or full-fat milk; driving lessons; satellite television; mobile phones; children.

Because the gin is there, and more bottles will keep arriving every other week or so, Julia has begun to take the odd glass in the evening. The taste, she assumes, is something to be acquired, a habit to form. After a couple of glasses the taste does not bother her too much. But she does not want to make this a nightly thing.

Despite the odd gin and the lighter evenings, Julia finds she cannot shift from the bedtime they honoured as a couple. Try as she might, her body clock tells her when to retire and she will drop off in her chair if she does not go to bed. Something similar must also keep Julia to her side of the bed. She had looked forward to spreading out, when ultimately she had the bed all to herself, but a deeper force keeps her in her regular, narrow channel beneath the sheets. Even if she manages to fall asleep stretched across the full width of the bed, she wakes up in her old place, facing the door, her back to the side when he had slept. There is no need to set a 7 am alarm now and, happily, Julia does find she can sleep later, past the alarm time, past that point when he used to launch himself out of the bed, grunting, farting, as he stumbled noisily to the bathroom.

Julia now likes to take a bath in the morning, usually with a book to read; it often takes up most of the morning. He always believed that showers were healthier and cleaner, so baths were discouraged. Julia runs her bath and adds a rose-scented product to the water. Some things are easy to change. Change for change's sake seems a stupid idea, but why not make a few small acts of self-assertion, defiance as she sees it, expressions of her individuality. Yet, she wonders too, how far is it getting her, to defy an authority that is defunct? Now and again it feels trivial and pointless. Julia sinks into the water up to her chin and does not look down at her body.

In the bath, and later as she dries herself, Julia is thinking about her forthcoming holiday in Spain. It is the thing that she has put all her hopes in: such a big step forward, something of her own. A packaged arrangement, of course; why take on too much, too soon? Still, each step in the research and booking

process has presented new challenges, new sources of
satisfaction: the passport; a wardrobe of clothing suitable for a
Mediterranean break; sunscreen; strappy sandals; novels
appropriate to read by a pool. This first, independent, holiday
would, almost ceremoniously, signal the start of a new life,
free from constraints, rules and retribution.

After her bath, Julia spends the day pottering about, a little
tidying, checking documents, looking at the weather forecast.
Finally she deposits herself on the sofa and waits, sipping her
gin (only slightly grimacing). Mentally she checks again that
all is ready and in order for an early departure: the cases in the
hall, the outfit for the plane; the see-through wallet with all the
essentials for travel and departure, including currency and
those little pills the doctor has recommended. She finds the
emotions she suddenly feels hard to decode and classify,
exciting certainly, novel, but also slightly disorientating. With
a flourish Julia finishes her drink and, suddenly feeling
vaguely precarious, makes her way upstairs.

Entering her bedroom in the gloom, curtains drawn, Julia
makes a slight stumble as she crosses the bedroom floor and
kicks the black bag that she has filled with his work shirts.
They all looked alike to her, those shirts, one or other maybe
differentiated by a slightly thicker stripe, but that could have
been an optical illusion, as she concentrated on making the
crease in the right place, when she ironed them. One shirt has
slipped out of the bag and onto the carpet. On an instinct Julia
stoops to retrieve it and in a practised motion she fits the shirt
to a hanger and returns it to the wardrobe. Once Julia has
done this, once the shirt is swinging, lonely in the wardrobe

and a hint of his cologne murmurs in that emptiness, there is nothing more for her to think about.

The next morning the taxi driver pips his horn at the time agreed, but Julia is still in bed. She is not asleep and is fully clothed. She does not know how to cancel the taxi. There is a knock at the door next, forceful, and maybe someone is shouting something through the letter box. The phone rings now, for many minutes. Julia remains under the covers, waiting for the coast to be clear. She gives it an hour, then rises, just at the point when his newspaper falls through the letter box. Julia looks around her. The bedroom is tidy, those black bags gone; the suitcases are back in the loft. Inside the wardrobe, her husband's shirts have been returned to their correct place, on their wooden hangers. Going downstairs there is a smell of polish and it is satisfying for Julia to inhale that conspicuous odour of regularity and order. The unencumbered sideboard has a deep chestnut glow to it.

Julia lays two plates at the kitchen table and takes out of the bread bin a fresh white loaf.

Based in East Yorkshire, UK, Ian Carass has worked mainly in education but is now devoting more time to writing. What interests him currently is the fable as a form and the themes of strangeness, loss and change. He is in the final stages of finessing a novel.

LAST NIGHTS OF THE PANTO

By Tabitha Bast

We usually wait until January for the panto, you can get seats close to the stage on the cheaper tickets. We take in our own snacks and drinks, to save money and save queueing. This year we were cutting back though, so we didn't go at all. I said that was fine, I was too big for it, just a shame for Ted because he's still little. That's what I said. But last year was brilliant, I laughed so much, I kept the leaflet as a souvenir which I usually do. Did. Last year was Cinderella and there was one fat ugly sister and one thin ugly sister, and when we had that terrible, enormous fight I shouted at my Dad that him and Mum looked like them.

That was really mean of me, and I'm older now, but, also, it was a bit true. My Mum is the fat one, and lying on her is the only way to get comfy on our shit sofa now. She's still got a bit of padding, but she's more like a square than a round. My Dad calls her Sexy Lego Lady when he's pissed and cheeky. My Dad is the thin one, he's tall and lanky and looks grumpy, like the BFG. My Mum says he's a secret fighter though I've never seen him brawl.

You wouldn't cross either of them to be honest, unless you're in their special inner circle which is just us and a couple of secondary characters. When I was as small as Ted it felt like nothing could ever hurt us. I know all kids feel like their parents are powerful, but this was different, this was actually because they almost were.

Maybe we don't need panto because my Mum is one all on her own. My best friend Kate - who comes back to our house most days - said she's like a cartoon, there's love hearts springing out her eyes when she likes you and thunderclaps circling her head when she's cross. When me or Ted do well at school and come home with some scrappy bit of paper proclaiming it her eyes turn into the seaside, tides of tears you get splashed with. And when we bump into Mr Morgan who gave me a detention back in primary school her expression is an entire audience booing him as she tightens her jaw, ready to floor him with her polite hello. That's how you know she hates you, she puts on her posh polite voice. It's a killer.

And then sometimes she gets sad. It used to be when it was her time of month, then she said it's her time of life, but now it just seems to happen all the time. Nothing has changed but somehow everything is harder at home, my Dad hasn't called Mum his Sexy Lego Lady in ages, they shut the kitchen door a lot even when they're not doing 'the things that matter'. They shut us out.

My Mum works for a union so when I come home from school the kitchen table is piled high with different bits of paper in various piles and there's always stickers and whatnot and depending on the size of the piles you can guess what sort of dinner it will be. I throw my bag on the bag chair regardless though she put pegs up in the hall that have stayed mournfully empty. When there's no room at all on that table I'll get to choose anything from the freezer to make for me and Ted, and we eat on trays in the living room. Those nights mean we can watch whatever, whenever. Mum's in there, eating cream crackers straight out the packet, radio on loud so you can hear the droney news voices proclaiming the threats of nuclear war and energy hikes and how bad it is and how much worse it's going to get. I don't know why she listens to that. Then she'll be moaning away to herself about her workload - or me when I creep in to see if there's pudding. "There's fruit in the fruit bowl" she'll say and if I don't go, she'll do that big resigned sigh and say "Okay check the treat cupboard" where there will be something way better. But if you ask her why she does all this work when its so much you just get told 'because it matters'. She says you have to always do the thing that matters. And then the next days, the piles get bigger and the door is shut more, and it builds up like a storm, as if the piles are sandbags to keep out the flooding, the door jammed closed the final defence, the radio an air siren... then I'll come back with Kate and Mum will be in a dark mood and fierce, proper fierce, ranting about the bosses and the government and we'll scoot upstairs as fast as. If you want water you just fill a glass up from the bathroom, don't go in the kitchen. But sometimes, oh god, the best times, when we come in and she grabs me off the doorstep and picks me up with her ox-like arms, shouts that we've won and, best of all, sometimes it means there is a takeaway tonight. Curry if I'm choosing, Chinese if its Ted.

As for my Dad, nobody understands quite what job he does. He's technically my stepdad but we're not bothered by that bit, he says we love and hate each other enough for the full range. We know Dad's clever but also he gets broken by very basic things; being hungry or tired; and he has to go running before work every other morning, like an overactive dog, or he's intolerable. Every few months he suffers a calf strain and there's two weeks of him at his most miserable and moping. Those weeks he goes to work cross and comes back cross but one hug; from me, from Ted, from my Mum; and he's kind again. It doesn't take much to bring him back from a place that feels very far away.

But early January felt like all the things had happened, that Mum hadn't won and Dad had a calf strain that couldn't be healed by a hug. It was hard for me too, because Kate was away with her family on yet another holiday and I didn't even have panto.

Ted cried when we got told, no panto. I laughed at him but Mum shot me that shut it look and I felt like a horrible uncaring person, like a boss, and I knew it was time for me to step up. I'd never quite felt this before but this was the first year it seemed like responsibility was on me to cheer us all. That we wouldn't get through January otherwise.

I'm too big for panto, but it's a shame for Ted. He's annoying, but he's my brother and he's sweet sometimes. So I started writing, and I got all the leaflets from all the Pantos we've seen over the years, the Aladdins, the Cinderellas, the Puss in Boots, the Jack and the Beanstalks, and I put them out on my bed and I sketched out some costumes and began a script. I couldn't keep it to the two of us, especially as Ted was so bad at remembering lines, but then I got all my old soft toys out from under the bed and gave them parts too.

Me and Ted, we worked for four days on this. I was like my Mum in her kitchen with all her tumbling towers of papers, but mine was piles of fabric and cardboard signs with funny dialogue on them, so Ted could hold up for our audience. This was strewn all over my room - bed, floor, and chest of drawers. I'd stuck a sign on my door for everyone to keep out. When Ted moaned that he didn't want to practice and why did he have to, I'd tell him that you have to do the things that matter.

I got Ted to make the invites on the second day, and they weren't very good but I told him they were. After I said that he got much better at his lines, and practiced all the harder. We'd shove my chest of drawers across my door to keep our parents out because I didn't have a lock and even with the sign saying keep out we didn't quite trust them to know we meant it. We'd watch some pantos on You Tube, then borrow bits for our script to make it funnier. I liked it best when Ted was absolutely roaring with laughter at his 'own' joke, even though he was just repeating what we'd just watched.

The night before the night before school we were ready. Besides, that's the date it said on the invites. We went to give them to Mum and Dad but we stopped at the top of the stairs. I felt a bit weird, a bit nervous. And Ted just grabs my hand with his sticky fingers and says "I'm excited, let's do it". I wonder if this is how my Mum feels, all weird and nervous and like it matters, and you can't mess up, you have to carry on regardless. If I had the money I'd totally get us a takeaway tonight.

The kitchen door is shut, we both see it from the top of the stairs and neither of us are sure. It means business, but we do too.

I squeeze his little sticky hand back, "Okay! Let's go!" and we steam down the stairs and into the kitchen where my Mum looks more tired than usual and my Dad, somehow, even thinner.

"Here" says Ted. He gives them the flyers. They're to be in the living room in two hours.

We power through the set up, and I make sure the curtains are closed properly, I'd 100% die if I got seen putting teddies in weird outfits around the living room. I think Kate would understand, but she's not my only friend, just my closest. You have the friends that understand and then the other ones. Luckily nobody would be snooping though because it's pouring down outside, there are big fat drops of rain on the window, it's so dark, like the whole street is saving on electricity.

We drag them in from the kitchen, or rather, Ted does, with those sticky hands, giggling, I stay put to get them drinks and snacks. They've got some regular looking wine just opened on the side that I pour into tumblers and I put basic crisps in a bowl like it's still Christmas. I'm looking for something better to feed them and I see the piles on the table and it's not the usual, so I have another look.

I don't understand why these are here, but there's no stickers. There's nothing saying fight back, it all just says pay. My

Dad's name on most of them, my Mum on others, and there's letters in red like Mr Morgan circling your spelling errors. There's loads of them, all crumpled, as if they've been once ignored, then fished out a bin and stretched out again, examined.

I take the drinks and the crisps in a bowl through to the living room.

Then we are on! I turn the lights down and switch all the fairy lights on, and I get this rush as if I'm brushing elbows with Chris Warton in Maths, and I shout at Ted - to his surprise and mine - "lights! camera! action!" and I look at the audience and my Mum and Dad, they don't look like superheroes, they look small and lost and perched on the shit sofa with bowls of crisps on their knees clasping their drinks as if that's all they have left.

It's not all they have left, they have us.

I'm not sure what I found in the kitchen, I don't think it's good. But I also know the show must go on. I think I have a bit of my Mum in me, like you win and you're back grafting the next day nonetheless or at least the day after if you've celebrated too hard. And I think I have a bit of my Dad too, that you need to get up and have a run regardless, that even if your work is something you can't quite put a name to, it's still important. It still matters.

"HELLO ladles and jellyspoons!" I shout at them, and Ted farts accidentally with a burst of a chuckle even though he's heard me say that before and then both my parents laugh too as if it's part of the whole event. My Dad leans back onto my Mum and her padding, he pulls out his phone to start recording, then thinks better of it and puts it down.

He puts his arm round my Mum's shoulders, tips his chin up and kisses her softly on her forehead, by her often furrowed eyebrow.

"Troopers, aren't they?" He says, interrupting our opening lines.

And then my Mum, right on cue, her eyes fill up with the watery goodness, like gravy for a roast, like a wine glass when you win. She fills up from nothing, magic, like a stocking at Christmas.

Tabitha Bast lives in inner-city Leeds, and works as a therapist and occasional writer. Writings range from political articles to fictional short stories.

FEARLESS

By Lesley Aldridge

I've had a 'no hitchhikers' rule, ever since the day my passenger suddenly produced a collection of rabbit skulls from his bag and proceeded to explain how each came into his possession.

On an undeniably grim day with a leaden sky and interminable drizzle, though, I feel compelled to break my rule and I pick up Will, who looks anxious and tired, with a half-hearted thumb out. He sinks wearily into the seat, gives me a watery smile and introduces himself.

I have a second rule, which states that should the first rule be broken, I will not be drawn into inane chatter, but I melt again on seeing his gloomy expression and ask him where he is off to. Will sighs and says he is rushing to be with his gran who rang a short time ago, upset that someone broke into her flat and stole grandad's military medals. Grandad died not long ago, he explains, and she has been polishing those medals every day since. She has nothing else worth taking, he tells me, with a melancholy shrug.

I feel indignation rise in me, and I say that surely the police can help with this, but he tells me with straightest face that she no longer trusts them since they refused to follow up the recent theft of her favourite gnomes. He adds that she didn't see the intruder, but as he escaped back out of the bathroom window, grandad's Yorkshire terrier, Monty, took a nip out of his hand. I smile and say that's something, at least. He laughs bitterly, "Yeah I guess".

Gran is pretty sharp it seems, and she spotted that his disappearing hand had a tattoo of a holly leaf on it. I silently admire her powers of observation and feel a quiet sense of satisfaction that the little dog stood up for his late master.

I hear myself say I will drop him at gran's if he directs me. He tells me I'm a legend, and eventually jumps out by a run-down maisonette and disappears nimbly up the steps to the door.

There's still just about enough time for lunch before my sales meeting, so I head hungrily to the supermarket in search of a sandwich. As the surly teenage boy in front of me hands cash to a motherly checkout operator, I hear her say,

"That cut on your hand looks nasty, you wanna get that looked at!" And, as I glance down at the injury, my heart skips a beat as I notice a holly leaf tattoo. He pulls his hand away and buries it in his pocket, red-faced at the unwanted attention. Suddenly I know just what I have to do, so I tell the bewildered cashier that I've changed my mind and dumping the sandwiches, I hurry out after him.

My heart is racing by now, but I catch up with him and call,

"Excuse me!" at which he turns round sharply, with a sour expression. "Yeah, wot?

I know if I have got this wrong I will seem like a frightening lunatic, and my courage almost fails, but I launch in bravely and say,

"We need to discuss what's in the bag," and I nod at his canvas backpack. He swears and goes to move quickly away, so I tell him hastily that I'm a police officer, and when he looks sceptically at my battered waterproof and chinos, I whisper "Undercover!" as my eyes dart around in an attempt to add authenticity to my claim.

He tells me in colourful language that this seems unlikely, so I go one better and say that I've been watching him all afternoon and that I'm aware that he is in possession of stolen military memorabilia. This is the killer blow, as his eyes widen and he pales and backs away.

Aware that he could certainly outrun a middle-aged man who has overindulged in real ale of late, and drawing on my encyclopaedic knowledge of TV police dramas, I tell him not to look round but there is an ARU in the corner of the car park, awaiting my signal.

"What's one of them?" he asks, by now clearly alarmed, and I explain that it's an armed response unit of highly trained officers ready to move in if he doesn't co-operate.

So I say, this is what happens next. We go back to the flat to return the medals, and I'll allow him to leave them at the door if he co-operates. Keeping what I hope is a severe expression, I tell him that if he doesn't do exactly as I say, my elite officers will move in swiftly and I add with sinister tones that there's no telling what Monty the Yorkshire terrier might do. He nods quickly, so I say into my cuff,

"All units stand down, for now" and I have a quiet inward chuckle at his relief.

I accompany him to my covert police vehicle and we set off. I can't resist telling him to check if anyone is tailing us, which he does with wide eyes, reporting that it's just an ice cream van. I say you can never be too careful, and swerve off to the right, down the road to gran's flat, as he breathes a sigh of relief and says we've lost Mr Whippy.

In a few minutes, we are right outside gran's flat. He scuttles to the steps and dumps the box, as I stand out of sight behind a tree, ensuring that he does what we've agreed.

At the very second he drops the box, I see the door suddenly open and Will leaps down the steps almost in one go, grabbing at the hood of the thief's jacket as he desperately tries to run. Holding him by the scruff of his neck, Will pulls his face closer to inspect him but as he does, the thief's flailing hand lands a sharp blow on his nose. Will staggers back, dazed, and the thief again tries to run, but this time I'm blocking his way and I put him in a headlock, as he swears and writhes.

Will is looking at me in utter confusion, but now seems not the time to explain how I came to apprehend the burglar, so I shrug and smile, as if this is something quite run-of-the-mill for me.

Suddenly I hear a shrill female voice cutting through the chaos

"What the hell is goin' on here?" Then as she sees the box, 'Ron's medals! Where'd they come from?'

We make a fine trio, Will muttering and catching clots of purplish blood from his nose, me sweating profusely and holding a scrawny teenage criminal and him, shouting at me in the endearing language I've now come to expect from him.

Once again he's incriminated by his tattoo as gran spots it and charges at him, brandishing a rolled up newspaper which she seems to have brought ready for combat.

For a split second I think that the only thing missing from this melee is Monty, but at that moment the feisty little creature appears, snarling and baring his minuscule teeth at the thief. Gran snatches him up before he has the chance to launch a further attack and suddenly she seems to have composed herself, as she calmly takes the box of medals, and with a small nod to me, puts an arm tenderly around Will and leads him back up the steps through the flimsy front door, banging it shut.

We're left standing awkwardly together as I release him, and I'm suddenly flooded with pity, so I say he really should get that cut seen to, and I remind him solemnly that we'll be watching him, from now on.

Lesley Aldridge grew up in Northern Ireland, surrounded by books and, with crossword and pun- loving parents, words have always seemed like fun. After a long gap, she took it up again recently and now she's hooked on creative writing all over again.

THE WHEELS MUST KEEP TURNING

By Warren Tang

It was big race day at the Happy Valley Racecourse. It was all the Hong Kong glitterati, foreign or home grown, could talk about for these past few weeks.

The wealthy Western industrialists, with their expensive tailored suits and wide smug smiles could afford to lose a few more thousand dollars betting on the gee-gees. They had cleverly financially exploited the fragrant harbour over the years.

Their wives did little else other than adorn their rich husbands' arms. The rest of their time was spent gossiping with the other girlies over cream teas, and maybe they would have the odd discreet affair if they could get away with it. Today, they couldn't wait to show off the new 'flapper' look fresh from America. Their short dresses, bobbed haircuts and brash behaviour was very appropriate.

Lam wasn't looking forward today. Lam didn't like the priggishness and contempt with which a lot of these race goers would display towards him. Rickshaw runners are considered the lowest of the low in Oriental society, the beast of burden in human form. However, needs must, and the continuous stream of fares was great for filling the glass jar at home. His dad Lee didn't trust the banking system or the authorities, not that there was that much to put away for them. It was from Lee that Lam had inherited the family rickshaw business.

Blood, sweat and tears have poured out of them in huge amounts over the years, but even with all that effort, it was only just enough to keep them barely on the right side of living.

It was not the kind of career anyone would dare to choose. Dealing with rude customers was one thing, the inhumane physical exertion in the constant bustling street din was another, but there was also the constant fight for road space. People walking, people carrying goods, folk on horseback, and recently, the increasing number of cars hogging the lanes. Lee foresaw the future. Worryingly, the more cars people were going to purchase, the less people would have a need for rickshaws. But he was doggedly adamant. While there was still a need for human powered transport then his rickshaws would be there. With the going rate being a mere 15 cents per mile, a lot of running and suffering needed to be undertaken to make it work.

Lee had literally run himself into the ground to raise the money to try to pay for the expensive medical fees, to keep his wife alive. His efforts were, ultimately, all in vain, and he has been bitterly resentful ever since. Lee wouldn't take another wife neither, it just wouldn't feel right.

Lam was only five years old when his mother passed away. He missed her terribly. His dad's strict tough love discipline was all he had known for his whole life. It would stand him in good stead, but only in the sense of drilling into him the necessary hard work ethic and determination that was needed in order to survive.

Lam didn't appreciate it at the time. He didn't always agree with his dad.

He had inherited his dad's whippet like lean physique, his fleet of foot and his stamina.

Lam, like his dad, never finished his education. The school fees couldn't be covered so the necessity for Lam to earn thereafter was all that mattered. Lam was only 14 and his grades were exemplary. During Lam's final year of full-time education, the school headmaster had noticed Lam's exceptional running ability.

He asked Lam if he would like to run in the annual inter schools' athletics meet. The school had no one to run in the prestigious boy's one-mile race. Lam simply shrugged his shoulders and accepted. He was too polite to decline his headmaster, nor did he really understand what he was agreeing to. It was explained to Lam that it was only four laps to get to the mile so his ordeal wouldn't last too long. If he won, the points he earned would help the school team.

Lam had asked his dad to come and watch but he wasn't expecting him to, such was the need to keep bringing the fares in, but come he did, albeit reluctantly. It would also be the first time that Lam would have run on a cinder track, or a track of any kind for that matter. Lee along with a few hundred others witnessed Lam win the one-mile race - by two clear laps.

If his dad was proud, Lam certainly couldn't tell. The headmaster on the other hand was glowing with praise after the race. He asked if Lam would like to represent the school in more meets. He had never seen such running talent in any pupil in all his years of teaching. Lee was immediately dismissive. He said that all it had proved was that Lam was more than ready to start pounding the streets to provide them with the much-needed extra income.

That was to be his last ever day at school. He was that hurt and angry inside that he couldn't speak to his dad for a good while afterwards. The big 'what if' question has hung over Lam ever since.

The very next day, Lam took his first rickshaw customers. It meant that father and son could work simultaneously, doubling the income. A cheap second-hand rickshaw had been purchased and primed ready for Lam.

"The wheels must keep turning", Lam was told in a not so subtle way by his father, "for us to stay alive, the wheels must keep turning."

And turn they did, day after day, week after week, year after year.

Lam's consistently faster cadence was very useful. He could get clients to their requested destinations quicker than the other rickshaw runners and sometimes, he was rewarded with much needed tips.

Other than sleep, there was very little time for anything else.

They would grab food whenever they could, usually from street vendors that were dotted at the kerb sides. Chinese barbeque pork filled baos or strips of fried dough were always their go to choices. Importantly, they were cheap and easy to eat while on the move. When stopping, they would seek out hose pipes or sometimes even fountains for liquid refreshment. Water is free after all.

It was utterly brutal. The tropical, stifling heat and humidity was unforgiving, suffocating. The clean white vests they would both set out in were quickly drenched in sweat and covered in dust and dirt in no time. There was no time for them to enjoy the sights, the sounds and the fragrant aromas like their passengers could.

It was like a desperate treadmill from which neither of them could get off.

At the end of each long day, they would return to the outskirts of the city to their small hut on what used to be the old family farmstead. For decades, spring onions, sweet potatoes and rice would be grown and sold at market. After all the other family members had passed away, mainly due to ill health and malnutrition, it was no longer viable to run the farm. Nobody else cared and they had to fend for themselves. The class system can be so cruel sometimes. The inferiority complex that had been ingrained with their ancestor's psyche many generations before and has since been passed down.

They were usually that exhausted after finishing their rickshaw shifts, Lam and Lee could barely speak to each other. Eventually, one of them would get up, the small basin would be filled and they would take it in turns to squat and wash themselves. They only had one precious bar of soap to use between them at any one time. They would then grab a few hours' sleep before the local rooster would loudly wake them both with the rising of the morning sun.

Occasionally, when picking up clients had gone quiet, Lee would indulge in smoking cheap roll ups. Lam wouldn't touch the stuff. Although Lee's restful puffs were few and far between, it was enough for him to end up with lung cancer. Lee's physical health took a sharp decline thereafter. He could no longer operate his rickshaw. It's been like that for a while now.

The pressure on Lam has been immense ever since. He wanted to earn enough to take his dad to get treatment, but he could never get close to the amount of money needed. His dad insisted that he would be fine. He told Lam to have faith in the traditional tried and tested Chinese herbal remedies he was taking.

While convalescing, Lee would reminisce about the first time he took out his young bride. Marriages were arranged but they struck lucky, they had fallen in love upon first sight. He had promised to take her to Victoria Peak with its beautiful panoramic view of Hong Kong. He had especially polished his trusty rickshaw until it shone, and added more cushions to ensure that she was comfortable. With power in his legs, and love in his heart, he enthusiastically set off. She felt so special and wanted.

When they got there, she was so struck by the stunning view. She was speechless.

In a rare candid moment, Lee revealed to Lam that he would love to go back there some time.

The big race day was in full swing. While some of the punters were getting lucky within Happy Valley racecourse, Lam himself got his own piece of luck when one of the clients gave him a generous tip. His first thought was for his dad, despite of everything that had gone on in the past between them. It meant that he could afford to take the rest of the day off and take his dad to Victoria Peak.

Upon seeing Lam coming home early, Lee had scolded him for missing out on potential money-making opportunities. Lam explained what had happened with his last fare and about wanting to take him to the peak. The barking had died down and Lee eventually simmered down when he understood what Lam had wanted to do for him. It is never the Chinese parent's way to apologise or to show easy generous gratitude, especially not to their own children.

For the first time in his life, Lee was actually the passenger in a rickshaw. He enjoyed the sights and sounds from the privileged vantage point, no one could say that hadn't earned the right do deserve this.

The steep climb to the peak a very tough one, but all the years of running and pulling clients along the hustling, bustling streets of Hong Kong meant that Lam was up to the task. His determination was further enhanced because he himself had never ventured there before either. The wheels had to keep turning not matter what.

When he arrived there, with dad in tow, his reaction was exactly the same as his mother's when she had first arrived there decades ago, stunned silence.

Lam angled the rickshaw to let his dad observe the view, to absorb it all in like he was.

After a few long moments of awe Lam said, "I see now what you mean dad, it was definitely worth it."

There was an unnaturally long silence.

Lam turned around.

His dad's eyes were shut, but he had a wide happy smile on his face.

The big wheel had completed its full rotation.

Warren Tang has been writing for 11 years, specialising in the Flash Fiction format. He was twice winner of The Cazart Flash Fiction competition, as well as shortlisting in other competitions such as The Word Hut Flash Fiction Contest and the Fusilli 200 Word Flash Fiction Competition.

FORTIETH

By Ed Walsh

Yesterday was a shock, seeing him at Shirley Lake. I had no idea he lived out there. I hadn't been that way in years and had only stopped to let the dog out of the car. It was at the north end where I saw him, where the trees and picnic tables are, and there was no one else around. It was a shock to us both.

"Judith?" he said. "It's you?"

"Dad?" I said.

"Yes, it's me," he said.

I had the feeling that if he had seen me coming from more of a distance he would have ducked into the trees. Maybe I had that feeling because I might have done the same if I had seen him earlier. Not that I hadn't been curious about what had happened to him, because I had. I had no idea about what became of him after everything that had gone on, he just seemed to disappear off the face of the earth. After seventeen years of seeing him every day, he was gone.

And I don't think the awkwardness was just to do with the time that had passed since we had last seen each other, or the way he had behaved then. I think he was also embarrassed by the way he looked. Twenty years before, when I had last seen him, he had been sporty; that was one of my main memories of him, him being fit and athletic-looking. He had been a county hurdler and we had trophies in the house. But when I saw him by the picnic tables he seemed to have shrunk and was walking in a slow and cramped way, like a small sea creature making its way across a beach.

He had also fallen behind in the clothing department. He used to care a lot about how he looked – they both did – and always took his time before he ever left the house. On their Saturday nights out, which were alternate, it used to take them at least two hours apiece. And they did look good, there could be no denying that. I had the best-looking parents of all my friends, and thinking back I suppose I was quite proud of them. Only Flo's parents came close, her father owned a gent's outfitters on our main street, Martin's for Men.

"You look good," I said, and he gave a determined little smile, appreciative of the lie.

"You too," he said. "You too."

"You living out here?" I asked.

"Not far," he said. "A mile or so."

He gave no more detail, so I assumed that that was about as much as he cared for me to know.

"You come here a lot?" I asked.

"Every day just about, five circuits. Keeps me looking good.' He gave the same smile.

Shirley is not one of the bigger lakes in the area, so I reckoned five circuits would take him an hour, maybe an hour-and-a-half judging from the way he looked. I wanted to ask more, of course I did, but I didn't know whether I wanted the answers.

"Is everybody ok?" he asked.

I guessed by everybody, he meant my mother and brother.

"Mother died four years back," I told him. "You didn't hear that?"

He closed his eyes and shook his head slowly.

"Sorry," he said. "I'm so sorry."

I got the feeling that he was saying sorry for more than my mother's passing. I didn't tell him about Robert, maybe he already knew.

He and Robert were close. We all were, but they had a special bond. Dad was the maths and physical education instructor at Robert's school, Delauneys, which was in the next town. They drove there together and came back together. They went to athletics meetings at weekends, some of which required overnight stays. Robert did hurdles and the long-jump, they were his specialities, although he could compete in most events without disgracing himself. So, all in all they spent a lot of time together and had a lot of laughs. We had no idea what they were laughing about most of the time, it was as if they had their own private jokes and sometimes a language we hardly understood. He called Robert Rob; to me and my mother he was always Robert. We weren't excluded exactly, but we weren't included much either.

So, standing there next to the picnic tables at Shirley Lake, and not having seen each other for so many years, me and my father quickly ran out of things to say. He stroked my dog and asked what he was called. I told him, Flake, and that seemed to take us into a dead-end. There was no swapping of numbers and arrangements to meet up. I just watched him shuffle off down the track and I felt sadder than I've ever felt before or since. I felt sad for him, and sad for me, sad for the whole damned world, just standing there under the bare trees in the November gloom.

When I got back, I wanted to tell someone about it. But I was living by myself then, just having been divorced for the second time. And it wasn't the kind of divorce where you stayed friends, the first one wasn't either. We got divorced because we had become enemies. I've always wondered about that, the people I know or hear about who stay friends with whoever they get divorced from. I think, if they stayed friends, why did they get divorced in the first place. I hear some say it's for the sake of their kids. Well, I don't have that problem, so we never stayed friends.

It never crossed my mind to ring Robert either, in fact I'm not sure I have a number for him now. I think he is in one of those rehabs where they don't encourage that kind of contact; one of those places where they seem to assume it was your family who caused all your problems in the first place, so it's best to keep them as far away as possible.

I don't usually buy that. I think there should be a time limit on how long you can go on blaming your parents for everything that goes wrong in your life. I think that, at twenty-five say – thirty tops – you need to start looking at yourself for an explanation for your troubles. Unless your parents sold you into slavery or something, I think you need to give them a break sometime, for their sake and yours. Things might have turned out the way they did – or worse – regardless of who your parents were or what they did. Most of its guesswork anyway - this caused that, that caused the other, someone went in for mass-murder because his mother didn't praise him enough. Well, maybe, maybe not. We all like our stories, especially the ones that let us off the hook.

With Robert though, I don't know. He took a big downturn when dad did what he did. He had been good academically, a bit of a maths whiz-kid, and was one of the stars of the athletics field. At the time, we were coming up to dad's fortieth and we were getting the place ready for a surprise party; nothing major, just near-relatives and a few friends. Flo, who was my best friend then, was helping out in the morning, putting up decorations. We had known each other from infant school, and had been in the same classes for ten years. She was at our place so much, people assumed we were related. She went home in the afternoon to get changed. The idea was that, when he came in from some meeting he had at the athletics club, we would surprise him. They weren't great friends with Flo's parents, but they were invited anyway because my dad was one of Mr Martin's best customers, and because me and Flo were so close.

There were about twenty of us and I was looking forward to it. Both me and Flo were seventeen and about to go off to different colleges, and I had the feeling that this might be the last time we would feel so close to everybody or to each other. We put some records on while we waited and Robert, who was fourteen then, made sure everybody had their glasses topped. Robert was a confident kid, and he got a lot of his confidence from my dad, just being his son was a boost to him. I remember Flo's mother remarking that he would make a fine husband for some lucky girl.

When it got to six and dad hadn't come back, my mother started worrying. Flo was late getting back as well and her parents got to wondering where she was. Her mother rang their house but there was no answer. My mother rang the athletics club but they told her he hadn't been there.

"What the hell's going on?" she asked nobody in particular, and of course nobody knew. So, the thing went kind of flat, people tried to keep some level of cordiality going, but with dad missing, and the Martin's thinking about Flo, it wasn't easy. People had theories – traffic on the ring-road, a flat, he must have bumped into a pal and was having a birthday drink with him. The Martins said Flo must have fallen asleep and that her room was a long way from the phone. I knew that wasn't the case, you could hear the phone from Flo's room. I don't know if, even then, I was the only one to put a link between my dad not being there, and Flo not being there.

Our phone was in the hallway and the place went quiet when my mother went to answer it. We could hear her say, "What?

What are you talking about Lawrence? I don't understand." She called him Lawrence, not Larry like she usually did. "Are you kidding me? Are you serious?" She laughed in an exaggerated way.

"Are you fucking kidding me?" I had never heard either of them use a word like that before. "No, you explain it now, not later. You can't do this" She put the phone down on the table and came back through.

"You need to speak to Flo," she said to the Martins. "Speak to your daughter."

"Flo?" Mr Martin said. "Where is she? What's going on?"

They both went through to the hallway. Mrs Martin shouted, "Get yourself back here, Florence, this minute." It was an occasion for full names, not Flos and Larrys.

"Florence, put Mr Binns on. We need to speak to him," Mr Martin said. Then he said, "Hi Larry, what's going on? We're getting kind of worried here."

He listened to something we couldn't hear.

"No, you're right, I don't understand any of that. Where the hell are you?"

He went quiet again. Everybody was quiet.

"Where? Where the hell is that? You get our daughter back here." Mr Martin didn't say anything for a minute, just listened, then, "I'm warning you, Binns, you get her back here. If she's not back here in thirty minutes I'm calling the police." We could hear Mrs Martin start to cry, and Robert ran up to his room.

The Martins came back in and nobody spoke at first. Then dad's brother asked what was happening.

"Happening?" Mr Martin said. "What's happening is your imbecile brother, mister God's-gift, has gone off with our daughter. Does that satisfy your curiosity?"

"Larry?" Uncle Bobby said. "Done what?" He looked at my mother. My mother nodded slowly, but didn't look as though she quite believed it either.

"Larry wouldn't do a thing like that," Uncle Bobby said.

"He has done a thing like that, and he'll pay for it," Martin said. "One way or another, he'll pay."

And seeing him out there at the lake, it looked like he had paid, one way or another.

Ed Walsh is a writer of as yet unpublished novels and occasionally published short stories. He lives in the north-east of England.

TURNING OF THE TIDE

By Wanda Dakin

I adjust the acorn-hard headphones in my ears and listen. The audible description blends in with the experience of my other senses: this beach. Here. Now. Encircling me. I feel the grains of sand on my upper back above the line of my swimming costume; the air a salty-seaweed tang mingles with the dense aroma of coconut sunscreen. Behind me, droplets of blood-red begonias, in neatly carved borders, and a board giving the sea conditions reminds me I am in France.

It is ridiculous, I think, to keep listening to the carbon copy when the real experience is right here. I rip out the headphones from my ears, put down my phone, and sit upright. The shadow of my elder nephew leans towards me, "Glace," he is annunciating, putting the fuchsia-coloured ice-cream under my nose, his mouth enormous in his small face.

My sister has got out her sunblock again and is smearing it over her younger son, Jack; he jerks about, the ice cream tilts on the cone like a globe, dripping down the side onto his dimpled hand. He stares straight at it, resolutely willing it to balance. His tongue emerges, as delicate as a rose petal, yet ferocious in intent. Sebastian, the elder boy, skin alabaster-white is set against curly dark hair, his eyes, a watery-hazel, drag down in his face.

"Auntie Amy, can you help me build sandcastles, please?" he tugs at my hand.

I feel the enormity of effort, like pushing against a boulder, just to connect with him.

"Come on, Auntie Amy, look lively," encourages my sister, Angela. Her very encouragement makes the boulder seem heavier, but I push the brittle plastic spade into the sand - too fluffy, useless for castles.

"We'll need to go nearer the sea to get the better sand," I tell him.

When we reach the heavier sand, Sebastian fills up his bucket; his brows pull together into a continuous black line as he turns it over. "Don't forget the magic pat," I say, and he gives it a fluttery tap, the air ruffles like imaginary birdwings. He lifts up the bucket slowly, his face decorated with expressions of deep contentment.

"Perfect," I affirm and build my own alongside; soon we have enough castles and start on the moat. Sebastian stands, hand on hips, with a look of 'what now?' on his face.

"We have to wait until the sea comes in," I tell him; then sadness rushes in like a wave as I think beyond that, to when the whole fortress will be destroyed. But Sebastian's mind will have not made that extra step, of that, I am sure.

We re-join Angela, Jack and our French cousin, Alain. Next week, Alain will return as a life-guard on these beaches. But now he is spending some time with us, during our holiday in the Pas de Calais.

I am watching the four of them playing football, with a familiar detachment, as if they are part of a dream. Jack is getting frustrated with his mother's skills, his eyes press intense like two grey buttons, "I want a t-u-r-n", he sing-songs.

"Well, you'll have to win the ball then," she teases. Frustration grips every fibre of his sturdy, three-year old body. In the end, in desperation, he gets hold of one his mother's leg;

Seb not to be outdone grabs the other. Meanwhile, Alain dribbles the ball away and kicks it into the makeshift net.

The boys are off, playing a new game. How easy to switch mood! Jack is laughing now, swooping in and out, arms aloft – they are playing aeroplanes. Jack seems to be pushing Seb into the shade, taking the small pocket of sunlight for himself; already it was happening, despite his three- year disadvantage, Jack asserting his superiority. Just like me and Angela, at that age, I think.

Angela has got out the picnic. Even the ritual of eating is conducted with zeal and precision. She neatly splits the baguette and puts a slice of ham in each. Jack, over-eager, drop his portion, grains of sand dust the bread like seeds. "Well, you'll have to eat it as it is, don't be so impatient next time." Jack knows better than to protest further starts to eat silently. At the end of the meal hand-wipes are passed round; then Angela turns to face her French cousin.

"It must be great, your job," she says to Alain, wistfully looking out to a dappled sea. Her small, thin nose is uplifted, expanding the two tunnels of her nostrils, as if she smells something delicious. In fact, it is just her way, in the uncomplicated world she seems to inhabit, to show unbridled enthusiasm.

"Rescuing damsels in distress," she adds nodding towards the sea. How innocuous it looks from any sort of a distance, folding over itself in tiny gasps. Alain puts his head on one side, maybe he doesn't understand the word "damsel", or perhaps he is hiding a darker side of his job. But he agrees reluctantly, "mais oui."

"Ames," my sister switches to the resigned tone of voice which she reserves for me," I take it you're staying here?"

She is on her feet again, shaking the sand from the orange beach towel, folding it in half, into quarters, replacing it in her small rucksack, leaving her hands free for the two boys. "But I want to swim, please Mummy," implores her elder son.

"The water is too cold, Seb. We're going to walk back with Uncle Alain to his house so we'll have a sea-walk."

"What about my sandcastles? Will the sea fill in my moat while we are gone?"

"Hmm," considers his mother. "I reckon high tide will only

just reach it. We'll be back in time". Then they are off kicking through the shallow water and immediately I feel the annoyance at myself; uneasy on my own, but not wanting to do anything either. Sighing, I tuck my headphones and phone into my handbag; an oblong packet stares back at me. I recall my recent conversation with the doctor, "These might suit you better. They should help with the anxiety too, but they'll take about two weeks to have any effect on the depression," the doctor swung round in his chair, simultaneously tearing the prescription sheet from the printer. His eyes looked weary, as if he was running out of options. In an effort to say something positive, I said, "the visualisation exercises are helpful – the beach one, in particular.

"Perhaps that might help – a holiday?" he replied.

Now, looking up, I hope that he is right. I notice that the sun has split the white cloud into two halves, just enough light to make a line up the beach and into the water. I am transfixed by the white pathway on the sand and rise to my feet, abandoning my belongings. I follow it downwards until the grainy sand gives way to a tough exterior.

Coming up from the sea's edge, with his windsurf, is a man who reminds me so much of someone else it takes my breath away: lean; straggly long hair; clear, remote brown eyes; the way he is smiling to himself. I think of him - tantalising, maddening elusive, Jase. The two of us lying side by side on the hill at Hambledon, sucked into the sky; for a moment together, then he was up, walking away. How he loved to travel, not so much for the culture or sights; but because he didn't have to stop, take stock of life. He didn't want children, ever.

I follow the white pathway into the shallow water, feeling the cool water wrap itself around my toes; in the sky, the sun finds new room to manoeuvre, diamond-shaped specks of light appear here and there, mesmerising me. Just like in the visualisation, the sea is calm, welcoming. I continue walking; the water is nearly level with my thighs ; it swills around me, teasing, friendly until I reach a sandbank. I walk to the edge of the sandbank and dip my toe-nail with its badly cracked varnish, over into the open sea. The white path still lures me, how easy to just keep walking, to let the water bathe me to sleep. The peace! I think of Jase again, or rather the shadow of Jase, trekking through Nepal; I think of my sister and the boys. I must be standing there for much longer than I am aware.

Beside me, I notice the sand staining a dark orange; I startle when I realise the figure of a slightly-built young woman, long dark hair wrapped around her cheeks. She is talking to me, warning me of the dangers of the sea, "Attention, madame, la mer est dangereuse." I turn round, but she has already left. The shore seems to have been pulled away from me, slightly out of focus

I put my feet into the water and am shocked that it comes up to my waist; beneath the surface there is a force that feels like giant fish, swirling around, almost tipping me off balance. I focus on the beach and pull my aching body through the fickle sea. So far removed from the shy, tentative lapping on the relaxation tape, the whole idea of it ever being such, suddenly seems ridiculously trusting. The sun has gone in and the sea reverts to a stern grey; once or twice the current takes me so strongly that I feel I will not recover, the coils of water press me tighter and tighter. Fleetingly, I think of Jase again, how I long to follow him into some warm new country. Is there still hope?

Just as I feel the last energy drain from me, the sun returns and the white pathway is back, guiding me to the shore; at last, the beach swills back into full focus. I bathe briefly in the luxurious rays of sun, once more the sea changes character, as if its temper is at last subsiding. It is then that I something, a rock perhaps, just a few feet to my left; then I realise it is not a rock at all, but the head of a small boy – Jack. When I reach him his small arms grip tightly to my neck, dragging at my head, he is crying but I have not the words to comfort him, all my effort is taken just to pull us through the water to safety.

By the time we reach the shore, Jack has stopped crying. His eyes, the colour of the sea, brighten, but they do not focus on me, but somewhere on the horizon. I see her running along the beach, eyes leant towards the trampled-down buildings and the blood-red streaks of begonias; her face is crumpled and one hand is stretched far behind her, clutching the hand of a dark-haired boy. My mouth shapes itself ready to call her name, but the word sticks in the air in front of me and melts. But then her head turns and she is running towards us; I let her younger son drop delicately into the sand; she scoops him up, her face remoulding with relief, joy, love. She is looking up now straight at me; her grey eyes soften with an emotion beyond gratitude.

My legs, tense with adrenaline, keep me from sinking into the sand. Later, I would feel a depth of fatigue such as I have never known before. But not the dragging weariness of depression, simply that arising from extreme physical exertion, mingled with an unfamiliar, sharp jolt of elation.

"Look, look at the moat," Sebastian is pointing at our creation, miraculously it seems Angela was right, the sea has only just reached it.

The four of us watch: the tide seems to be going out again. At that moment a pocket of sea mist brushes away the sun and swills along the sand, wiping us out, then leaves us again, to the slowly declining day.

****

"I was distracted," Angela explains later. She was apologising to me, to Jack and mother-kind in general for her negligence, "distracted by the ramblings of some strange young French woman. She came up to us; we were nearly back to the point we left you."

"She was proper weird," agrees Seb.

"I kept telling her to slow down, 'lentement, je suis anglaise.' But my French isn't up to your standard, Amy, all I could understand was something about a woman being in danger. She kept saying, 'sur la motte de sable'. I tried to calm her down, but I noticed Jack was missing. Seb and I should have really been wearing our glasses then we might have spotted him."

'La motte de sable', I translate in my head, of course, sand-bank. And I am shocked, not for the reason behind my smile. Just that I have remembered how to smile at all!

Wanda lives in Gloucestershire with her husband and rescue dog. The inspiration for Turning of the Tide came from holidays in Northern France when her children were young, and on one occasion they got caught out by the tide.

FLASH FICTION

BABY LOVE

By Ellen Evers

I am held with my face close to creased papery skin that smells of unknown things. I've never made old age and I wonder if this time I will know what it's like to have lines and aches and pains. Rheumy eyes peer and a voice says, "I do declare, he's been here before!"

There is laughter and I know it is time to smile my gummy smile for Great Aunt Lucy as everyone 'ahhhs'. Shaky arms plop me on a shoulder where hands pat and rub my back. I reward the doting watchers with a rich burp that delights the room. Someone comments that I will not be allowed to do such things as I grow and I know this is true.

I tire of all this passing to different smells; I only want Mamma. She is a lovely Mamma; I can remember so many who were not. She is warm and soft and she loves me I know. Mamma rocks me and I can feel the delicious drowsiness that follows a feed. I'm drunk on milk. I smile again; it's better than any cheap bourbon.

I have been here before; actually, I've been a baby before not in a family like this you understand but I've been given a last chance to redeem myself. This time all the cards are in my favour. All I have to do is to behave and lead a decent life. Sounds easy enough in a place like this, doesn't it? I'm a rare soul who has deep memory, not many do. It will remind me of the pasts I've endured. Aunt Lucy is talking now. She's very old and has no children and more importantly no grandchildren. I have wooed the old lady with my baby charm and she is smitten with me. She tells them this afternoon that she will be leaving me all her wealth as I'm the baby who will carry the family name. I beam with joy and they laugh.

"He knows what you're saying Aunt Lucy," trills Mamma obviously delighted at the news. I give one of my rare but perfect gurgles that send them all into coos of pleasure.

"Of course, when your next babies come along, then Alfred will share with his brothers and sisters." I do not reward that comment with a smile or a gurgle. My parents gaze fondly at each other. They intend more children! I would have to share my inheritance which I do not want to do.

I decide there and then that the peaceful nights they have enjoyed so far would now be shattered. I can scream like a banshee when needed. They would not have time to make any new babies, nor will they want to with me as an example. Aunt Lucy's money would be all mine as promised. I have entered the world with good intentions. I must not fail again.

I decide to practise my wailing ready for the long nights ahead.

Ellen is a seventy-something retired teacher from Cheshire who enjoys writing short stories and non-fiction When she's not writing she likes walking and keeping fit, being with my family and lots of travel. She loves history and enjoy being a tour guide which sometimes inspires her writing.

JACKSON CREEK

By Gail Warrick Cox

When I was a little girl, my momma told me never to go to Jackson Creek, and so I never did. My Daddy had departed in '29, I barely knew him, but I did know he left Momma and me wanting. Consequently, I always tried to do my best and never add to Momma's troubles. Anyways, it seemed more of a place that boys would frequent, not nice young girls like myself and my friends in our white cotton dresses and soft ribboned hair.

But when a Southern Belle blooms, she is not quite so inclined to follow her momma's rules. And so, one hot and sultry July evening I broke from my convention and joined a group of giggling girls intent on skinny dippin' at Jackson Creek.

It was more beautiful than I had imagined, and I could not comprehend why Momma had forbade me. The glass green water pooled lagoon like where weeping trees trailed their tendrils and vibrant dragonflies darted in golden sun. Toward the rear of the pool water flowed fast and white over jet black rocks with a rushing sound as it gathered pace and headed for the mighty river beyond.

The other girls were already down to their flimsy slips, laughing and squealing at their abandonment of all things proper. I let down my hair and unbuttoned my dress, it slid to the grassy bank. I unclasped my brassiere and breathing deeply took in the earthy aroma of my surroundings. I was liberated. I plunged into the pool kicking and splashing with the other girls, our spirits high as gliding eagles, our skin a tingle amid the icy water. But soon the cold cramped my legs and stole my strength, the current pulled me to the rocks and although I shouted for my friends they could not hear above their laughter and the rushing white water.

I sank. Rigid with fear and unable to move a column of bubbles escaped my nostrils. I knew I would need to take a breath soon and when I did bitter green liquid would surely fill my lungs. Hope had all but abandoned me when somethin' truly magical happened. Strong arms embraced me, guided me gently to calmer water where my friends spotted a limp body and dragged me coughing and retching to shore.

I never told Momma of my ordeal and I never went back to Jackson Creek. In time the memory faded and life progressed.

Darlin' Momma passed away this fall and on going through her treasured belongings I came across a faded newspaper clippin' the headline just so:

Local Businessman Missing Following Wall Street Crash

And now I tell my own little daughter never to go to Jackson Creek. I expect one day she will defy her nagging momma as all young people do. But I take comfort, for I know, deep beneath the rushing white water her Granddaddy waits to save her. Just as he saved me, from the perils of Jackson Creek.

Gail Warrick Cox lives in Dorset, UK where she enjoys beach walks, reading, time spent with family and friends.

OKAY TEACHER!

By Oluwatimilehin Oladiran

When I grow up, I'd graduate with honours in astronomy, flaunting to friends who joked life would spit me. I'd never go up though, I fear black holes: I'd work on the ground. Hopefully, Tesla's still accepting CVs from men like me. Black, queer, and proudly effeminate. I don't think they would; I think I'd offend the more conservative generation so I'd either hide all my piercings or write research papers from my semi-dirty apartment.

By the time I'm thirty, I'd regret picking astronomy as a major and dabble into writing: cursing my father for forcing me into this course. I'd move from Florida to New York, meet a Broadway director who'd scream in joy at the brilliant musical in my hand and announce to theatre heads that he's found the next Lin-Manuel or at least Michael Jackson.

I'd own a workshop, have a dancer boyfriend; I heard New York's much kinder to gay folks: I'd move my parents from Nigeria even though they hate me; I'd move them from their murky bedroom and rub my queerness in their face whilst still begging them to accept me, whilst still hoping my mother would stop disturbing Jesus with gay prayers.

Eventually, they'd accept me, hopefully, and I'd write another musical, on coming out. Like all cheesy writers say on even cheesier channels: "My work is a part of me, my characters are the expression of my soul." I'd finally have the liberty to say that, it would finally be true as flowers are tossed from the elevated platform of Rogers and Hammerstein, and tears fall because it's finally happening.

By the time I'm fifty, I'm as prominent as Stephen Sondheim. People would celebrate my birthday with parades and open congratulations on news channels who don't really care but feel obligated to shout "happy birthday."

My friends would include Kristen Chenoweth, Patti LuPone, Cole Porter (hopefully alive by then), and Daniel Radcliffe (hopefully gay by then). We'd have tea on our porches, bathe in vodka, and read Shakespeare at parties. At seventy, Tesla would be looking for me; they want a successful astro-scientist to grace the cover of one opulent magazine, and I'm successful, although not by astro science. I'd take the offer, not because I want to but because my publicist is excited. Out of luck, a hero who saved the planet is on the magazine.

Late shows would ring, radio interviews would knock, everyone wants to know what he's like, what it felt like working with him and although all my life I tried running from homophobia, fate whirled me hard because the man hates me, even more than he hates his gay son. I'd go to the grave, guilty, or at least in question as to whether I should have laughed with him, as to whether I betrayed my community.

But first, before the inescapable tragedy of my life begins, I must finish this essay on where I see myself in fifty years.

Oluwatimilehin is from Nigeria.

A COLD CONDOLENCE

By John Blair

"She hasn't passed on; she's dead as a dog." I refocus on my steering through dense traffic upon the snow-packed streets.

"Show some respect," Joanne says. "If not for the dead, then for my poor sister at least."

"Your sister is not even related to her."

"She adopted Felicity. You know Franny sees her as her own daughter. How can you be so cold?"

"I dunno. Maybe because it's freezing out?"

Joanne says nothing more, and I don't mind the silence for the rest of the trip.

Inside the funeral home, we shake the snow off ourselves and hang up our coats. Joanne's wacky family has gathered, looking mournful and lost, consoling each other, hands on shoulders and backs. The air is stuffy and warm, and I'm sure I can smell the chemicals they use to preserve bodies.

We step into the room. I glance at the pictures on the wall; bloody boring black and white prints.

Cheap affair. I can't wait for the sandwiches afterwards, so we can eat, and then bolt from this craziness. The barely audible piped-in violin music certainly adds to the sad mood.

A small group of people has lined up to see Felicity. I creep up behind Joanne and whisper, "An open casket is a bit much, don't you think?"

"I'm not talking to you."

She grinds her teeth; she knows I hate that.

"No ceremony for me, please," I say. "When my time comes, just cremate me."

"That might be sooner than you think."

Got to admit, that was a good shot she just gave me; I struggle not to smile.

Blubbering, blue makeup running down her plump red face, Franny waddles our way from beside the coffin and throws her arms around Joanne.

"We're sorry for your loss. Aren't we, Robert?"

I nod absent-mindedly. "Yes, of course."

Franny lets Joanne go and stares at me.

"Hello, Robert."

Trying to think of something nice to say, I point at the casket. "Well, she had a full life."

This starts Franny bawling again and another relative rushes over and gives her a big hug.

We leave them in a corner of the room, and I roll my eyes.

Joanne says, "How could you?"

"What? It's not as if Felicity ever liked me."

"You never gave her a chance, the way you ignored her all the time."

"Listen, it was her time. We all have to check out when our number's up."

"Sometimes I wonder why I married you."

"Good looks? Charm?"

"If you're trying to be funny, it's not working."

"Listen, darling," I try to be serious. "Get a grip. Felicity was pretty old."

"Only twenty!"

And she plucks a piece of tissue paper from a box on a nearby table.

"Good God." This time, I've reached my limit. "She was just a cat."

John Blair is a fiction writer and high school teacher in Toronto, Canada. His most recent novel, Hockey Camp Summer, is available from Amazon. John continues to write whenever possible, with help from his cat Felix.

TILES

By Patsy Collins

I lock the door as though I care whether anyone knows what I'm about to do. As though someone might care enough about me to come looking.

Naked on the toilet, I surrender to this decaying squat. Warm water fills the bath. Jason wired us into the hotel next door's electric supply that time he was clean for a while. Now he's wired up to machines and everything his body needs to keep it alive comes in through a needle, just as did everything which brought him to that living death.

No half measures for me. There's a sharp blade waiting to set me free from this hell. Sharp enough anyway. My raised hand brushes antique art deco tiles. Pretty but for the cracks and scum and stained grouting. The mirror which might have shown me something else was pretty once is in another room. Put to another, beautiful on the surface, use. Where it no longer hangs the paint is fresh and bright.

This place was cared for once. This room, this house. Loved once, perhaps but now the weight of its sagging roof threatens to crush the thin walls. It groans a quiet plea for help. Too quiet. Its windows are boarded up, its doors locked, its facade unwelcoming. A metaphor?

I unlock the door, fetch bleach and phone my mother. Whilst the water cools I scrub the once pretty tiles. Maybe if I get them clean enough they'll be worth saving.

Patsy Collins spends her time making things up and writing them down from her home in Lee-on-the-Solent, England, or whilst traveling in a campervan. When away she enjoys scrambling round ruined castles, visiting friends and eating cake. At home she gardens, bakes (and then eats) cakes. Learn more at patsycollins.uk

POETRY

ODE TO AFFLICTION

By Aisling McEvoy

I fell in love with misery,

The darkness at my door.

It puched me til I gasped for breath,

And then I asked for more.

I'd watch it through the window,

Waiting for the day,

That misery would swallow me,

And take it all away.

I took a chance on hope.

It'd come to me in waves.

But it'd migrate like the swallows,

Then I'd feel nothing for days.

I turned back to anger,

It made me feel okay,

But when the feeling split my bones,

I found another way.

My last friend was numbness.

It took me by the hand.

Together we watched the waves crash in.

They found me on the sand.

Aisling McEvoy is from Laois in Ireland. Writing became something important to her during lockdown. She usually writes short stories but loves the freedom poetry gives her. She is so excited to be included in this volume's anthology.

THE LITTLEST WITCH

By Dawn Rae

The Very Big Witch has a broomstick

With bristles that stick out all over.

The Nearly Big Witch has one also

Which she rides from Darjeeling to Dover.

The Middle-size Witch has a yard broom

Which gets her from A to B,

But the Littlest Witch has the dustpan broom

So she has to walk, you see.

The Very Big Witch has a cauldron

That holds enough brew for a year.

The Nearly Big Witch has a ten-gallon drum

(But her brew tastes a little bit weird).

The Middle-size Witch has a potjie-kos pot

And her brew does knock out the bunch.

But the Littlest Witch is the littlest

So she has to stick to fruit punch.

The Very Big Witch has a BIG spell book

With spells to suit any occasion.

The Nearly Big Witch has some nasty spells, too,

And will use them without hesitation.

The Middle-size Witch will throw spells around

Whenever it enters her head,

But the spell books are heavy for Littlest Witch

So she reads Enid Blyton instead.

The Very Big Witch has a wart on her nose;

One eye is green and one blue.

The Nearly Big Witch has scraggly grey hair

Which she likes to dye red, white and blue.

The Middle-size Witch has fingers like twigs

And the biggest feet you could get.

But the Littlest Witch is as pretty as pie.

Still, she's little – there's hope for her yet.

Dawn Rae hails from Cape Town, South Africa. She's written many poems and stories and currently has four ebooks available on www.kobo.com. Dawn would love to hear from you at dawnrae.author@gmail.com on Twitter @DawnRae1611, Instagram with dawnrae1611 and Facebook as Dawn Melodie Rae.

SILENCE

By Emily Raisin

He has a voice as soft as his soul,

As soft as the air on sand,

As soft as his pink and open palm

That holds the grooves and curves

Of the lands.

He has lips - so gentle -

That can blow the dawn's golden song

From the rivers of his mellow palm

That quietly stream along.

He has a heart that holds the beats

Of the creatures running in the grass,

And his lungs are filled

With the sound of the stars

As they smile together and laugh.

He looked at me

And with soft fingertips

He made the whole world quieten.

And said,

Just listen.

And listen I did,

To this beautiful man called Silence

Emily Raisin is a young British writer from Lincolnshire, United Kingdom. She draws a lot of inspiration from nature and humanity's relationship with it. Her current projects include her Instagram poetry page @post_itpoetry_ and her debut novel, which remains a work in progress.

VEGETAL WOMAN

By Kenzie Packer

Glimmer pools from windows, out of the mansion of the heart,

To stir with the bottommost remains, what remains—

A risen vision, spectral, wreathed in bay and laurel and thyme,

Folded and baked, a sprinkle of the dirt completes:

The Vegetal Woman, cultivated from their prayers,

A bowed head like magic that un-bows elders of the grass.

Give them the spell, the charm, the incantation to move beyond,

Give not to me spell books but gateways, already carved with runes.

Kenzie Packer is a New York-based writer currently studying Dramatic Writing, English Literature, and Creative Writing at NYU. She is enchanted by words and the ways in which a few of them strung together can transform minds, spur emotions, and awaken the unseen parts of ourselves.

BIRTH OF A NIGHTINGALE

By Ece Karadag

A Nightingale was born

in the pitch black of night.

The mother of this Nightingale

sang peacefully day and night.

But that day

Her mother began to sing

the lament of eternal grief

with her delicate voice.

The birth of the Nightingale

was a harbinger of death

and grief, but the only

truth was she was cursed

by their master

they named God.

The Nightingale swore
not to sing peacefully
after her mother's
eternal grief.
The Nightingale had a
thicker and
more frightening
voice compared to
the others.
One day her mother
died suddenly and
the Nightingale started
to sing the Victory
March, which was
written by God with
the crimson blood
of her beloved mother.

A PRAYER TO BABBITT

by Fiorella Ruas

Please allow me silence in loneliness

And purity in peace.

In all that I see.

Please allow me not to see

What I don't want to see.

Please allow me to stay

And listen to the sea

And think with the waves in my ears.

Please allow me not to hear

What I don't want to hear.

Please allow refuge.

A silent beginning.

A smile in my words.

Please allow me not to say

What I don't want to say.

Fiorella Ruas' writing background is in theatre. After one of her plays received critical praise in the National press, she was commissioned to write for Film and TV. Fiorella has just finished her first novel, has always written poetry but up to now, never tried to get it published.

TO BE HELD BY LIGHT

By Lesley Mason

(after Linda Hogan)

To be held by light,

to be airborne and

seeded by raindrops,

to float on a

trusting wind;

To follow the unseen

path to the wisdom within,

the sacred space, the

healing place;

To walk alongside the beautiful

ones, and the damaged and hurting,

the ones who help and the ones

who need to be healed;

To be held by the light

is also to hold the light,

to swim through the rapids

rather than to simply be

carried forward on the turbulence

of this white-water world.

Based in the UK's "city of stories" (Norwich), Lesley is embracing retirement, working towards a simpler, slower life, having acquired a new home, nicer neighbours and beach hut along the way. Among her mantras: Words Matter, choose them wisely, use them kindly. And focus on the good stuff.

THEN CAME

By Gee Parkinson

First came birth, innocence, joy, laughter

Craving togetherness, yearning to play, learn

Then came anger, hostility, quarrels, trauma

Victim of violence so young, longing to escape, be free, happy

Then came bitterness, blame, confrontation

Ready to retaliate, challenge, win

Resuming weakness, suffering, vulnerability

Dominated, controlled, abused, betrayed

Then came freedom, new beginnings, friends

Support, love, unity, opportunities

Suddenly blinded by charm, wealth, charisma

Exploited, influenced, oppressed once again

Then came endless torture

Emotional mind games, history repeating

Downtrodden, timid, worthlessness

Hungering for a lifeline, a way out,

drowning in guilt, failure, diffidence

Then came a strong, independent woman

Respected, proud, unaffected no longer

Grateful, empowered, self-reliant and successful

Finally feeling safe, needed and loved

Then came birth, purity, deep affection

The need to nurture, protect, keep safe

No more harm, hurt or upset

Just the indescribable sensation of mother love!

Gee Parkinson grew up in South East London where she graduated with a BA (Hons) in Creative Arts and now lives in Somerset with her daughter. She worked for over twenty years as a teacher before turning her hand to writing, due to significant events that happened in her life.

WORKING NINE NINE SIX

By Creana Bosac

Chamomile, valerian, lavender:

I call urgently for

your services. I need

a dusty green glass flask,

cork-stoppered, care-labelled

in apothecary's sun-faded script.

I reject now a life of nine to nine

six days a week, craving

free time, identity,

my deep-night phone scrolling

stealing sun from darkness,

self-time from sleep, from dreams, from sanity.

It's over now but how do I relieve

the pain, reset the strain

of sleepless nights, of days

packed tight like bitter pills?

In this modern, harsh world,

I call again the remedies of old.

Chamomile, valerian, lavender:

please help me now.

Creana Bosac is from Leicestershire, UK, where she has worked as an Associate Lecturer for the Open University and now edits and writes creative writing critiques. Having written mainly scientific documents before, she is enjoying writing creatively and has had a number of pieces published and shortlisted in national competitions.

THERE'S STILL TIME TO BE CREATIVE?

By S.R Malone

Sunlight stings my eyes,

Reds and oranges bleed through lids

too heavy to open, at first until

steaming coffee is introduced.

Train is late, arrives cold like an animal

in from the rain. Ticket costs double,

who wrote the code for this machine?

Weary-eyed, propped up by caffeine,

we paid.

Painted-on smiles for the department on arrival,

All lingering through a sterile, cold open-plan,

Dread, fading energy, fading hopes.

Will there be time, later on, to be creative?

Work through lunch,

Sandwich wrapper tossed in the wrong recycle bin,

Don't forget to rinse it off.

There's still time to be creative, yes?

The train has been cancelled,

Dead carriages linger, a forty-five minute wait

in a draughty station,

There's still time to be creative, yes?

Murky twilight ebbs on the horizon,

Lulling heads judder against the shaking panes

of a bus navigating chaotic traffic.

There's still time to be creative… possibly?

Blast-fry a pre-packaged meal,

Sunlight replaced by dusty lampshades

and the fluorescent glow of television screens.

There's still time to be creative, yes?

But wait. Now. Now's the time?

When the world is folding in on itself,

And production ceases, save for fast food outlets

and hospitals. Now is when that connection

can be forged?

NOW it's time to be creative.

You still have the energy, yes?

No, don't close your eyes!

Sunlight stings my eyes.

S.R Malone is a writer based outside Edinburgh, Scotland. He is primarily a science fiction writer, inspired by a steady mix of classic literature and old movies, coupled with the unescapable urge to put pen to paper.

STARFISH

By Heather Haigh

You promised to make me a star

If I shone brightly enough

For you

No backbone

No brain

All limbs to embrace you

Maybe I should be

A star of the sea

Go with the flow

Let you drown me

Sink me

Drag me to abyssal depths

A starfish

For a cold fish

Should I be a common starfish?

One of many

A trinket

Hang me from a tree

To be admired

Judge my shape

My colour

My symmetry

Or perhaps a crown-of-thorns starfish

A queen is allowed to be prickly

Touchy

You see

Starfish can be mothers with others

Or mothers alone

Perhaps I'll find my own way

Teach my daughters

You don't need

To shine

Heather is a disabled, working-class writer, from Yorkshire, UK who found the joy of writing late in life. Her words have been published by: Reflex press, Horned Things, Black Moon Magazine and others. She likes to make and wear silly hats. You can find her at @HeatherBookNook.

WE NOW ACKNOWLEDGE

By Sandra Achebe

The fragrance of your emergence

   ...Births along ambiances

Amidst nostalgias of a flowing fondness

   …Trapped in verses weft

And sprinkles of ink on air.

I am your muse with echoing's from our fathers,

Surrendering oddities

Of the house that built me

For out of this house

Springs up a collage of greatness.

Regale us onwards

In metrical verses

Feed us with words of orchestrated symphony

Playing us the rhythm of your labyrinth

That our memories maybe filled with your writings.

Oh dear one

I fear of thy indulgence

Of intricacies wherewithal

Convoluted from a voice soft as gale

And ripping as a sword.

These piping's of melancholic dance

To defiant practices unsought,

If words the path will resolve

Drown us then in verses

Drunk from the fount of your words.

Sandra Achebe is a Nigerian writer, poet, resource speaker and creative educationist. An exceptional muse to humanity her works have appeared in Rubies Africa, The Kalahari Review and elsewhere. Her chapbook 'Before the clock strikes 12' was listed among the winners for the 2020 PIN (Poets in Nigeria) Chapbook series.

UNTO THE WATERS

By Sarah Edwards

The cap twists easily

as a soft breeze lifts

then streaks my cheek

with a powdery kiss

your last

I bend low

over the clear waters

mountain-cold

unsullied

such purity shocks

takes my breath away

then takes you too

in furling eddies

your boneless being

weightless

untethered

no past

no now

into the known unknown

my gaze yearns

stretches

then blurs

reflected in the limpid flow

it shimmies

pools

vanishes in your wake

shock's edges soften

purity caresses

your kiss I taste

a breath I take

Sarah is a Londoner living in North Wales. Writing for her is a form of meditation, an escape from the outside world. She writes about instances that provoke a strong emotion and about the little things in life that often go unnoticed.

SKY

By R.J. Finnerty

The woe never leaves,

Ever-changing, never grieves.

O' the wings that soar

When the darkest cloud calls to pour.

And that light is lost;

I await its return.

Two minds aloft for

A debt I did not earn.

The present be my prison,

Life just a wait.

For no other ear to hear

Of my sorrow, my pain, or my hate.

Ryan is relatively new to poetry, but has long enjoyed creative and descriptive writing. He likes to convey what is often unsaid and find the beauty in the binaries of the world. He lives in London.

PHOENIX

By Finlay J. Goodwin

You have made me lose hope;

you have made me fall to despair.

And now, by the edge, I see the slope

seeing life undressed and bare,

leaves fallen, colours broken,

division spread, love left for dead;

And now I know what I must do.

Ride atop life like an aged mare,

Make from the branches a new yoke

Though it is broke, soon gone, forsooth

And through despair rise up as one

Ready to take upon it all,

with the helmet of truth I don

Now knowing how to stand upright,

for every time I fall.

Finlay is a Cambridge student studying English, who grew up in Doncaster, in the UK and he finds great purpose in writing whatever comes to mind.

PHANTOMS

By Ursula O'Reilly

Is that the wind whining,

Gnawing at my door?

A woeful spectre calling,

Silhouette lingering?

Or merely phantoms rising,

In my coffee cup?

What is tap- tapping,

Upon my windowpane?

Storm raging, or a beastie

From the olden days?

Perhaps an ancient banshee,

Calling for the dead?

I shake away the notion,

Only the squall, I say.

The shrieking tempest's fury.

Feline yowling for a mate?

Or merely phantoms rising,

In my coffee cup

Ursula O'Reilly is a writer/artist living in Ireland. Her interests include painting, and drama. Ursula's work has appeared in various literary magazines including: 'Dawntreader Magazine', 'Vita Brevis Press', and 'The Literary Yard'.

ONE

By Louise Hastings

I am pure love.

That's the only message worthy to hear,

The only truth to drown out the fear,

I repeat it over and over to fill and surround me with light,

So I can see clearly my path in the night.

I let love fill my wounds and make me whole,

Calming my mind, my body and soul,

Allowing them to align and become one,

One with the universe and to shine bright like the sun.

For that is why I am here; to shine brightly my light,

Triumphing over darkness, loving over fight,

Forgiveness over bitterness, gratitude over indifference,

Choosing caring and sharing for a life of magnificence.

Thank you brave, brave heart for all you have done,

I love you unconditionally, may we always be one.

ALL-CONSUMING NIGHT

By Amelie Addison

There will come a time when it all goes dark, they say,

No you, or me, to see the day.

The sun will run, and leave an expanse of dark,

An inky blackness cold, desolate, and stark.

So bathe in every sunset, absorb all the light you can,

Before we return to the darkness whence the universe began.

Live in every moment, find joy in all places,

Be consumed by love for your people, their faces.

To be blank and empty is not for you,

The stars will implode and give us that hue.

You must feel alive in every way you can understand,

A smile, a laugh, the touch of a hand.

It'll all come to nothing, no dawn in the east,

The cosmos entire, finally released.

An expansion of galaxies proves too much to handle,

The last star's light wavering, as if from a candle.

And that light will flicker and weave,

The thing that has bound all humanity will carefully leave.

And the all-consuming night will stretch out to forever,

You, and me,

Stardust together.

Amelie, is from the U.K. and is inspired to write to make sense of the world in her own way.

PERSPECTIVE

by Faith McCormick

How does one focus on one problem at a time

When one's troubles are endless and large?

Eating an elephant is no small task

Mother insisted you take things bite by bite

I find that I feel different now that I am on my own

Sometimes to devour the largest land animal

You simply need the right knife.

Published in 2022 by

The Anansi Archive

The Anansi Archive is an online community of writers supporting each other's literary endeavours.

If you would like to join this project please email

info@anansiarchive.co.uk

or visit the website at

www.anansiarchive.co.uk

If you have enjoyed this book, tell others about us.

Get the word out.

Printed in Great Britain
by Amazon